Si~~~~ ~~~~nuchion

Sin and Seduction

Emma Allan

LIBRIS

An *X Libris* Book

First published in Great Britain as *The Pleasure Principle*
in 1996 by X Libris

A CIP catalogue record for this book
is available from the British Library.

ISBN 0 7515 3067 0

Typeset by
Derek Doyle & Associates, Liverpool
Printed and bound in Great Britain by
Clays Ltd, St Ives plc

X Libris
A Division of
Little, Brown and Company (UK)
Brettenham House
Lancaster Place
London WC2E 7EN

Sin and Seduction

Chapter One

'WELL?' NADIA ASKED impatiently as soon as they sat down.

Angela grinned broadly. 'Well,' she said on a rising inflection. 'Where shall I start . . .'

A young, slim, curly-haired waiter arrived at their table. Nadia saw Angela's eyes roaming his trousers inquisitively, the way she always did with any man who was even vaguely attractive – and even with some who were not.

'What may I get you?' he said in a clipped precise English, avoiding, Nadia noted approvingly, any unctuous reference to their gender.

'Champagne cocktails for two,' Angela said.

The waiter nodded and walked over to the bar at the far side of the room. They were in the River Bar of the River Hotel overlooking the Tower of London and the Thames. The room was decorated in dark blues, with pictures of London river scenes on the walls. Comfortable armchairs, upholstered in a lighter blue, were placed around small burr walnut tables like the leaves of a quatrefoil. Nadia had selected a corner table though the bar was not crowded.

1

'Go on . . .' she urged. 'I want to hear all the gory details.'

'Perhaps nothing happened,' Angela said teasingly, the tip of her tongue between her lips.

'Not with that smirk on your face.'

'Perhaps he swore me to secrecy.'

'That's never stopped you before.'

'Well, the dinner was great.'

'Where?'

'Gavroche. *Soufflé Suisse*, *Canard Pot au Feu*, *Tarte Tatin*. Fourchaume Chablis, Cos-d'Estournel and . . .'

'D'Yquem.'

'How did you guess?'

'Modest little meal.'

The waiter returned with their drinks. He set two paper coasters, emblazoned with the hotel logo, on the table and sat two elegant crystal glasses on top of them. He added a trisectioned silver dish, its handle shaped into a fish, which contained pistachio nuts, black olives and little pastries stuffed with anchovies.

'Take those away, please,' Angela said at once. 'If you leave them I'll eat them.'

The waiter turned to see if Nadia agreed. 'Madam?' he queried.

'Yes, take them . . .' she said, a little surprised to be asked. Angela's personality was usually so forceful her demands were met without question.

'Will there be anything else?' he asked, scooping the silver dish back on to his tray.

'No,' Angela said, smiling at him sweetly, 'thank you.'

'Cheers,' Nadia said, picking up her glass.

They clinked glasses. Angela Barrett took a long

sip then settled back into her chair, crossing her legs. She was an attractive woman. Her red hair was her most striking feature, a red like a sunset, an iridescent colour cut into soft waves that fell to her shoulders. Her face was striking too, with emerald green eyes, their whites as clear as fresh snow, a large but well-proportioned nose and a fleshy rich mouth. She was slender and radiated health and fitness, everything about her body taut and well exercised. Her legs, which she flaunted in short skirts or skin-tight leggings, were long and shapely. Tonight, though she'd come straight from work, Angela was wearing a black Mani suit, its skirt displaying a great deal of thigh which was sheathed in sheer black nylon.

'So, obviously he asks me if I'd like to see his flat. Well actually he said apartment. But he is American.'

'And?'

'Did I tell you we're in his chauffeur-driven limo?'

'Naturally.'

'Well, the chauffeur takes us back to this building off Davies Street. Modern place, all black glass and stainless steel. He's got the penthouse.'

'Naturally.'

'It's massive. I mean rooms the size of a croquet lawn. I swear he's got two Picassos and a tiny Chagall and that's only in the hall.'

'And in the bedroom?' Nadia sipped her champagne, watching the bubbles eating away at the cube of sugar in the bottom of the glass.

'In the *sitting* room . . .' Angela insisted, ignoring her friend's interruption, 'there was a beautiful Edmund Cropper. He said it reminded him of his home town.'

'Can we cut to the chase,' Nadia said impatiently.

'Vicarious living?' Angela joked.

'Angela, you know that. If it weren't for you I wouldn't have any sex life.'

'It's sad, isn't it?'

'Very. So?'

'So. So I ask him if he's going to take me to bed. You know I don't like beating around the bush.'

'Did you want to go to bed with him?'

'Of course I did. He was gorgeous. He looked like Rossano Brazzi in *South Pacific*.'

'That dates you, doesn't it?'

'I saw it on television at Christmas. Anyway I was wet for him all evening.'

'Angela!' The shock was only feigned. Angela did not mince words.

'Well it's true.'

'What did he say?'

'He looked at me all serious, like he was going to tell me the meaning of life. He asked if he could trust me.'

'Trust you?'

'I said, of course he could, trying to be serious too. Then he goes all quiet. Gives me a glass of this wonderful Armagnac. He still looks serious, as though he's trying to make up his mind about something. I just stare back at him all wide-eyed, wondering what on earth's going on. Then, suddenly, he tells me he thinks I'm a very provocative woman.'

'Provocative?'

'He says he's a very rich man and that very rich men get used to having their own way in life. He says that he has got certain needs, certain special things he wants, very private things. Of course, I'm totally intrigued by now. My imagination's running riot. Then it's like he's made up his mind. He tells me he's sure he can trust me and he's looking at me with this really intense stare.'

'I'd have run away.'

'Don't be silly. Curiosity killed the cat. He takes my hand and leads me down the hall. It's a special room, he says. I mean, I'm imagining faked-up dungeons and whipping stools and mediaeval racks. So at the end of the hall he opens this door. The room's completely black – walls, floor, ceiling, everything. No window. There's a single divan dead centre lit by two spotlights overhead. It's covered in a black sheet. And there's a table, like an altar table against one wall with two massive white candles on either end. If there'd been a pentagram I'd have thought he was into black magic.'

'Weren't you scared?'

'No. He was harmless, Nadia.'

'How could you tell?'

'I don't know, just something about him. Anyway, I was fascinated. I wanted to know what he was going to do. Well, he asks me to take my clothes off, just like that, no kisses, no hugs. He had a lovely voice, very soft, like chocolate mousse. It made me shiver. So I ask him to unzip my dress – you know that yellow one with the spaghetti straps. He just shakes his head. So I do it myself. His eyes never leave me for a second, not a second. I'm only wearing stockings underneath, no knickers, no bra. There I am standing in my high heels and hold-ups with his eyes boring into me. And I'm throbbing. I mean palpitating. So I kick off my shoes and peel off my stockings.'

'And he's still dressed?'

'Oh yes, he's just standing there in his Huntsman's suit and Dunhill tie. He asks me to lie on the bed, on my back on the bed he says, and I do as I'm told. It's only when I lie down I realise the sheet is silk, really incredibly soft silk. He comes and stands over me, looking down at my body and for some reason I'm in a terrible state. My nipples are so hard they feel like cold steel and I swear I must be soaking the bed. And he hasn't even touched me. Must have been the way he was looking at me. Then he goes to the table and I hear him undressing. I could have twisted around to watch but for some reason I knew he didn't want me to. When he comes back he's wearing a short black robe embroidered with some sort of oriental serpent in red and gold. I can see his legs and they look strong and muscled. But as far as I can see he hasn't got an erection. He's carrying a black sheet, like the one on the bed. He flaps it out over me. It covers me completely apart from my head. I can see my nipples sticking out through it. He says very quietly that I must try to be still, as if I were in a very deep sleep, then he slowly draws the sheet up over my face.'

'That's creepy.'

'Creepy but exciting. The silk feels delicious against my body. So I'm lying there with the sheet over my face and I can't see a thing. I feel his hand tracing the contours of my cheek and jaw and down over my collarbone. Well, by the time it gets to my nipples my whole body's trembling. He just strokes them one after the other through the sheet. And I'm going crazy, moaning and gasping and only just managing to keep still. My clitoris is throbbing like a vibrator. The silk feels like oil against my skin, like I'm covered in oil. It was such a peculiar feeling.

What he's doing to my nipples drags the silk up and down all over me.'

'God, Angela, you're turning me on.' Nadia felt her own nipples stiffen in sympathy.

'So his hand eventually moves down to my belly. To tell you the truth I think I'd already had one orgasm just on what he did to my breasts. By the time he's got his hand on my thighs I'm completely soaked. I can feel it. And I'm squirming around like a fish, can't help myself. He puts his finger down between my legs, just one finger, pushing the sheet down with it and finds my clit instantly. I feel the silk working against it. And he's so good. What he does is perfect. Well, I'm coming again in seconds, really coming, screaming and moaning, writhing under the sheet, which only makes it worse because the silk feels so wonderful against my skin. He starts to push down until the sheet's dragged between my legs and I can feel him pushing it right up inside me. I'm so wet it's effortless. He puts his finger right up into me, covered by the sheet and, at the same time, his other hand is on my belly, another finger on my clit. It's amazing. I'm coming over and over again. Suddenly I hear him moan – well, cry out really – like an animal, a really strange noise. I feel his hands slip away. So I raise my head and the silk falls away and he's standing there with the robe open and the sheet is spattered with his semen.'

'But he had both hands on you.'

'Exactly. Spontaneous combustion.'

'Weird.'

'You can say that.'

'So what did he do then?'

'Like nothing had happened. He just leaves me in there. I get dressed and wander back into the living room. He's sitting there in a tracksuit with a glass of Armagnac and starts to talk about his investment portfolio. Just like it hadn't happened.'

'You can certainly pick them, Angela.'

'I know, but I'd never have guessed he was the type. The strangest thing was it turned me on so much. I mean, I was buzzing. Unbelievable.'

'Perhaps you've always had a thing about silk sheets and didn't know it.'

Sometimes Nadia wondered if the stories of the sexual exploits Angela came up with were, in fact, figments of her vivid imagination. But Angela was never short of suitors and it was equally possible that the outlandish details were perfectly true.

'Anyway, the chauffeur takes me home in the limo,' she concluded.

'Are you going to see him again?'

'Who knows? He's got my number.'

'And if he rings? Will you go?'

'I'll think about it.' Angela could not suppress a shiver. 'I might, I might not,' she said, grinning.

Nadia attracted the waiter's attention. She made a sign that they wanted another round of drinks and he nodded that he understood.

'You seem to attract them like a magnet.'

'Who?'

'Men who aren't the full sixpence.' Nadia had been friends with Angela since they worked together as graduate trainees on an accelerated promotion scheme operated by a firm of stock-brokers. They had shared everything, talked through every affair, every liaison and Nadia's disastrous marriage.

'I don't.'

'You do, Angela. You've had more than your fair

share. What about that guy who asked you to beat him with a school cane?'

'That was fun. He never called me again, though. I think I gave him more than he bargained for.'

'And the guy with the fur.'

'That's only two. Most of the rest have been normal.' Angela liked men. She had a voracious, almost masculine, appetite for sex. As she had never found a man who could satisfy her rapacious demands over the long term she had never been tempted to settle down. She liked all the games. She liked the variety. She liked the thrill of conquest – the female, in Angela's case, definitely taking the predatory role.

They talked about other things over their second drink, then divided the bill and left the slender waiter a five-pound tip. Angela had to go to the first night of a new opera at Covent Garden where the financial services company for which she worked was using its permanent tickets to do some corporate entertaining. As Nadia lived in Islington she offered Angela a lift, her car, a Mazda convertible, having been consigned to the hotel doorman.

'Are you going to the exhibition tomorrow?' Nadia asked as the doorman retrieved her car from the forecourt and drove it to the front entrance.

'What, the Jack Hamilton?'

Nadia slipped the doorman a ten-pound note as he held the car door open for her, then he raced round to do the same for Angela. They climbed in. 'You got your invite, didn't you?'

'Oh yes, but I've got Yamatso coming in at six. He usually wants dinner at Harry's Bar and brandies at the Dorchester. I can't do it. And I really wanted to meet him.'

Nadia pulled the car into traffic. 'Who?'

'Hamilton. Didn't you see him in the *Sunday Times*? They had him stripped to the waist. He's a hunk. Pumps iron and runs. Believes in the Greek ideal – healthy body makes for a creative mind. Well, he can have my body any day. And he's got these come-to-bed eyes . . .'

'Angela, you think any man under sixty has come-to-bed eyes.'

'Come on, I'm very selective. But he's really something.'

'Well, that means I'll have to go alone. Someone from the company's got to go – we're sponsoring it. Gordon can't, he's in Hong Kong.'

'Is he still on the board?'

'Retiring next year. He's the only one interested in art.'

'Sorry I can't come.'

'Can't be helped.'

Nadia dropped Angela at the bottom of Bow Street and drove around the Aldwych. The traffic was heavy but fluid and in fifteen minutes she was home. She had put down the deposit on the flat-fronted Georgian house three years ago with the proceeds from her first big bonus. It had been expensive but one of the advantages of working for a merchant bank was fixed and low-rate mortgages.

Nadia opened the front door, deactivated the burglar alarm and climbed two floors straight to her large bedroom and en suite bathroom which occupied the whole second floor. She had spent a lot of money having the house rebuilt to her specifications and the bathroom, in marble, had cost her the most. It was worth every penny.

Turning on the powerful shower, housed in its

own cubicle, Nadia stripped off her clothes and let the strong jets of water wash away the alcohol-induced tiredness that had suddenly seized her. She climbed out of the glass stall and into a white towelling robe, staring at herself critically in the large mirror behind the double wash-hand basins. She was thinking of Angela and the procession of men she managed to troop through her life. In contrast she had recently had only desultory relationships with one or two males, whom she cared about neither socially nor sexually.

She was no less attractive, she thought. Her flaxen blonde hair was expertly cut in layers and neatly framed her face. She had a small, slightly retroussé nose, high, sculpted cheekbones and a perfectly symmetrical mouth. Her lips were naturally a deep ruby red and her eyes a blue that had reminded past admirers of cornflowers. Nor was her body any less spectacular than Angela's. She was slender with a narrow waist, full hips and abundantly curved buttocks. Her legs were long and finely contoured and her breasts full and firm and very round, riding high on her chest in defiance of gravity.

It was, of course, nothing to do with appearance. It was a question of personality. Angela was outgoing to the point of being outrageous. She had no problem with going up to a man in a bar and asking him to buy her a drink, nor for that matter asking him to take her home to bed. Nadia had never been able to operate in that way though she had began to wish, especially after her divorce, that she could. Not that men were slow to approach her. She had enough offers, but they were frequently offers from the wrong men – men who were too old, too boring or too married, the last category

11

predominating. Had she been prepared to settle for an affair, to become a man's mistress, she could have chosen from a dozen candidates. But she was not.

She had done so once, and once was enough. After her divorce she had been courted by one of the senior partners of another merchant bank. He was elegant, worldly and sophisticated, all the things that her ex-husband was not. He had taken her to the opera and bought her little gifts of jewellery and clothes, all from the finest shops in Bond Street. He had made love to her with passion and enthusiasm and élan. He had told her he was married but Nadia thought she didn't care, that she would be able to cope with being merely his mistress, called on to perform whenever he was available and his wife was not. And for a while she had coped well, until one evening she had seen him, quite by chance, out with his wife, sitting in a restaurant where Nadia had arranged to meet a client. Suddenly the cosy accommodation she had come to with herself, the lies she had told herself and all the little deceptions they had practised on the pretty brunette she now saw for the first time, seemed sordid and despicable. Moreover she realised she loved the man and that her most profound emotion, as she watched the way his wife smiled and laughed and so clearly cared for him, was jealousy. It hurt her more than anything else had ever hurt her and she swore that was one mistake she would never make again.

Her divorce was not on the same scale of tragedy. She had married the wrong man for the wrong reasons. She had married a man with no ambition or drive because she wanted to be married. No other reason. She wanted to be married because it was like an insurance policy against the failure of her own career. As soon as it had become apparent she was not likely to fail her needs had changed. She had hoped he might change with her, that they could jointly bring a new dimension to married life, but it soon became apparent he was not willing to oblige.

Fortunately he had been tempted by the delights of a nineteen-year-old telephonist at British Telecom. Nadia and Doug's sex life had never been more than perfunctory. She was more interested in her career than sex and was glad that Doug appeared to be satisfied with very little. When he'd announced he wanted a divorce, her first emotion was relief, followed quickly by astonishment as he took great pleasure in telling her of his sexual exploits with Sharon, whom he had fucked and sucked and nibbled comprehensively, in every conceivable position in every possible location. With Nadia the limits of his endeavour had been the missionary position every Friday night.

Since her divorce, and her married man, Nadia's attitude to sex had changed and she found herself yearning for the sort of sexual adventure Angela apparently enjoyed. It wasn't that she hadn't had lovers. She had chosen one or two and they had been competent. They had performed adequately, indulging in foreplay and holding themselves back until she'd had her pleasure, as befitted a New Man. But she had hardly been driven wild, thrashing around and panting with lust. It had all been carefully controlled, calculated and, in the end, distant. And now, at this point in her life, Nadia wanted, and needed, more.

Wrapping the robe more tightly around her, she went down to the kitchen to make herself some tea.

13

She wasn't hungry. She had had lunch with a client at the Pont de la Tour. She sat at the breakfast bar in the kitchen and sipped a mug of strong tea. Once again Angela's story had left her restless. She glanced at the paper to see if there was anything on television that would distract her but there was nothing. She kept seeing an image of Angela stretched out under a black silk sheet being caressed by Rossano Brazzi.

Almost reluctantly Nadia walked back to her bedroom. It was nearly dark and she closed the cream curtains on the two large windows that overlooked the street. She didn't turn on the light. The gloom suited her purposes. She took off the robe and hung it on the back of the bathroom door. There was a tall mirror in the bedroom and she stared at her naked body. Her nipples were erect. She looked down at them. Their flesh was dark, a cherry red, and jutted out from the thin band of areola that surrounded them. She took her breasts in her hands and squeezed them gently.

'Damn Angela,' she said aloud.

She wondered if she would have become so concerned with sex if her friend hadn't regaled her with her sexual exploits quite so regularly. Was she just trying to ape Angela in some way?

Nadia lay on the bed. She had masturbated rarely in her early days. Now she found it more and more necessary. The strange thing was the more she seemed to need it, the less satisfactory it became. Her body was like a rarely played musical instrument. It was not capable of the demands made on it and did not respond well. Not only was her body out of tune when it came to the desires of her mind, she felt she did not know how to play the

14

instrument to its best advantage. Perhaps in truth masturbation was not to be her forte.

She could see herself in the mirror. It was immediately opposite the foot of the bed and she scissored her legs apart so the whole long crease of her sex was visible. Her pubic hair was soft and quite thick on her mons but did not extend down between her legs and she could see every detail of the deckled scarlet opening of her vagina. It seemed to be smiling at her, a mocking vertical smile.

She began to stroke the soft fur of her pubis, still debating with herself whether she should be bothered. As her finger nudged against the top of her labia she felt her clitoris pulse weakly, as if it too could not decide whether it was worth the effort to join in.

On impulse Nadia rolled over. There were two small chests of drawers on either side of the bed, in one of which she kept all her lingerie. She opened the bottom drawer and extracted a black satin slip. Lying on her back again she draped the slip over her body and raised her head to look at the effect in the mirror. The satin smelt of her perfume. She always kept her empty perfume bottles in the lingerie drawers. She could see her hard nipples sticking up under the material.

Closing her eyes she rested her head back on the pillow, inhaling her own scent. It smelt musky, more like an orchid than a rose. She could feel the silky satin against her body and remembered how Angela had described her experience. Was this how she had felt? What would it have been like? Her clitoris pulsed more strongly, deciding it did want to join the ceremony. She imagined Rossano Brazzi standing over her, stooping to circle her nipples with the palms of his hands, a knowing smile flickering over his face.

Nadia opened her legs. The hem of the slip was covering her pubis. She pushed the silk into her labia and found the cache of her clitoris. Delicately she rubbed it from side to side with the silk, and felt it respond with a frisson of pleasure. Her body moved almost unconsciously against the satin. Just as Angela had described, it felt deliciously sensual against her skin. Her clitoris pulsed strongly. She pressed it against the underlying bone, trapping it with the silk, then dragged it up and down. A wave of sensation made her shudder.

Closing her legs tightly she rubbed the tip of her thighs together so that her labia were trapped too, the satin caught between her legs. She could feel her wetness, leaking from her body. In the darkness of her mind she saw a big, circumcised erection edging towards her, a tear of transparent fluid escaping from the little slit that seemed to resemble an eye. It did not belong to anyone. It was anonymous and disembodied. It throbbed visibly, blood coursing through it, the glans smooth and pink in contrast to the shaft that supported it, which was rough and veined.

She eased her legs apart slightly to give her finger room to work on her clitoris. The spectre of the cock loomed large. Nadia imagined holding it in her hand, squeezing it, feeding it into her mouth, taking it in her throat, sucking it so hard it swelled even more. She imagined it pushing into her labia, testing her wetness, delving into the silky, pliant cavern of her sex.

What caused the change she didn't know. Suddenly the cock was not anonymous any more. It belonged to Doug. On the screen behind her eyes she saw Doug's body on top of her, remembered how she had looked up over his shoulder and watched his big, fleshy buttocks rising and falling as he drove his penis into her. He had a permanent pimple on his left buttock and it had often fascinated her. She had the feeling that it changed colour as he pumped away, fluoresced from pink to red, flashing like a lighthouse, a code in Morse she did not understand.

The thrills and trills of pleasure from her clitoris were lost. She manipulated it harder but only caused a wave of discomfort verging on pain. She tried moving her finger against it with the most delicate of touches, using the now wet satin, but that produced no feeling at all. It had become dulled and insensitive. It had no power, no dominion over her body any more.

Like a deflated balloon Nadia felt the excitement seeping out of her. She opened her eyes and looked at herself in the mirror, tearing the black slip away angrily. With both hands she grabbed her breasts, squeezing them hard then pinching her nipples, trying to get her body to respond. But all she felt was pain. She released them, white finger marks momentarily impressed on the pink flesh.

'Damn you,' she said aloud.

Chapter Two

IT WAS CROWDED, so crowded it was difficult to see any of the pictures. They had not been roped off and the small gallery was so full of people they were practically touching the canvases. Not that anyone appeared that interested anyway. Most were there to press the flesh, to network among the critics and the journalists and members of the Arts Council who attended the event, or simply to gossip and grin and hear the latest news in the chattering classes. The champagne flowed copiously, and waitresses in short black uniforms circulated with trays of canapés that had been warmed and rewarmed so many times they had started to congeal and melt into the paper doilies on which they had been arranged.

She spotted him through the scrum. He had found a little corner at the back of the room and, even among so many, gave the appearance of being on his own. He was not quite as dark and brooding as Nadia had imagined from Angela's description, but she was certainly right in every other respect. He was a deeply attractive man.

A big buxom woman in a bright orange dress invaded the private space he had created and buttonholed him, trapping him against the wall. Nadia watched as the woman talked at him, emphasising her monologue with sweeping gestures at the various paintings. He had black hair, thick wavy black hair which fell, like a comma, over his forehead, occasionally brushing his bushy eyebrows. He would flick it back with a toss of the head. His eyes were the colour of burnished mahogany, a liquid mahogany that seemed to express an understanding of the profundities of life, and were, also, it seemed to her at least, etched with a kind of sadness.

He was tall and had the relaxed ease of someone who is happy with their body. He possessed a natural poise and grace of movement that was underlined by his obvious physical strength.

Excusing herself from the little group of people she had become attached to, Nadia squeezed her way towards Jack Hamilton through the crush of people. He saw her coming and fixed her with those eyes as she manoeuvred through the minefield of wine glasses and paper plates. As she got nearer she could see the eyes were quizzical. She read the question as 'What do you want with me?' and wasn't sure she knew the answer.

The buxom woman was talking earnestly, undeterred by Jack's obvious lack of interest. 'So I always see these things as a matter of form, not content, don't you agree? Oh look, there's Patrick. Do you know Patrick Proctor? He's wonderful, don't you think?'

'Yes,' Jack replied noncommittally.

'Must say hello. Excuse me, won't you . . .' And she bustled away.

'Hi,' Nadia said, taking her place. 'I'm Nadia Irving.'

'Hi,' he said with no enthusiasm.

'Aren't you enjoying yourself?'

'Would you?'

'It's your show.'

'You saw my picture in the catalogue.'

'Yes.'

'Not in the *Sunday Times*?'

'No.'

'Good. That bloody article has plagued me.'

'I've heard about it.'

'I should never have done it.'

'Why did you?'

'Pure foolishness. So what can I do for you? Please don't ask me some silly question about how I see the artistic process or why I only paint in oils or who my models are. If I could explain what I do I wouldn't have to paint.'

'I wasn't . . .' Nadia floundered.

'What then?'

Nadia couldn't think of a single thing to say. She had come over to him because he was the most attractive man in the room. She could hardly tell him that.

'I just wanted to tell you I thought your work was striking.'

'Striking! Well, that's a new adjective at least. Have you actually seen it?'

'Yes.'

'Have you? How can you in here?'

'I work for the company that sponsors the gallery. I saw the pictures at the preview last week,' she said assertively.

'I'm sorry,' he said at once. His eyes softened and

he smiled gently. 'I really am. I hate these dos. You spend three years of your life trying to say something, trying to do something and nobody even bothers to look at the pictures.'

'I looked. I think you're good, very good.'

He was. Hamilton's work was mostly figurative and he painted with almost photographic realism. But he had an ability to convey a mood and an atmosphere that suggested not only the situation in which his subjects found themselves but much wider issues. There was a resonance that spoke of the human condition, that touched a chord, or should have done, in anyone who cared to look.

'And what do you know about art?' The words were full of resentment again. He wanted to use her to prove a point to himself – that nobody understood what he was trying to do.

'I know I need to get an emotional response from a picture. I know when I find a picture moving. I know when I don't.'

'And you find my pictures striking?'

'I find two very moving indeed.'

'Do you? Which two?'

'The woman in the turquoise dress and the little boy with his mother.'

Jack Hamilton suddenly looked straight into her eyes. A broad grin broke over his face and he started to laugh. It was as though she had passed a test, a rite of passage to his respect.

'Absolutely right. The rest don't really work. But those two – I can't paint better than that.' His eyes continued to stare into hers, looking at her now as if to see into her soul. 'Can I get you another drink?'

'No, thank you.'

'So, Nadia . . .'

The words hung in the air. Despite the way he had treated her initially, or maybe precisely because of it, Nadia felt as strong an attraction for this man as she had ever felt in her whole life. She could feel her heart pounding and her pulse racing. And then, quite suddenly, she knew what she had to do.

'I don't suppose you would like to take me to bed, would you?' She had never said that to any man before, and never dreamt she would be able to. In fact, it came quite easily.

He grinned again, but with no smugness. His teeth were very white and regular. 'I'd like that very much,' he said quietly.

Nadia's heart was beating so rapidly it felt like a bird fluttering in a cage. What was she doing, what on earth was happening to her? She was mimicking Angela. But she realised immediately she had no regrets. She felt suddenly free and in control in a way she had never experienced before, as if heavy chains of restraint had fallen away.

'Would you like to go now?' he said conspiratorially.

'Don't you have to stay?' Was she hoping he would say that he did? She hadn't expected him to act so quickly.

'I don't think so. I've done my duty.'

'All right.' And she found it was all right.

With a gentleness that belied his obvious strength he took her by the elbow. It was the first time they'd touched. They were going to bed together and they had had no physical contact. Strangely the idea thrilled her. He led her through a small exit at the back and, in two minutes, they were standing outside on the street. Ten minutes later, courtesy of a black cab, they were drawing up outside a small mews off the Fulham Road. The staircase of the mews was on the outside and he led her up the stone steps.

'My studio,' he announced as he opened the door.

Nadia walked into a large open space with windows set into the roof. The room must be wonderfully light during the day, she thought. To one side was a fully fitted kitchen and at the back, an alcove containing a double bed.

'Drink? Booze? Coffee? Tea?' he asked.

'No thanks.' Nadia had kept her mind in neutral during the journey, trying not the think about the implications of what she had done.

'Do you do this often?' he said.

'Do what?'

'Pick up strange men.'

'I've never done it before.' Her sincerity was obvious.

'Why's that?'

'I've never wanted to.'

'I'm flattered then. Why me?'

There was a big chunky sofa against one wall and he sat on it, inviting her to do the same. The studio was not what she might have expected, had she had time to think about it. It was not wild and untidy and dirty, but neat and well ordered and clean, everything in its place, canvases and materials racked and stacked, and books carefully shelved. There were bright coloured rugs on the stripped wooden floor. The white walls were covered in pictures but, in terms of style at least, they appeared to be the work of others.

'Could I change my mind?' she said as she sat down next to him.

'About what?'

'I'd love a glass of wine.'

He got up immediately and went to the kitchen. 'White or red?'

'Red, please.'

He took a bottle from a wine rack set under one of the counters and opened it, taking two glasses from a wall cupboard.

'So why me?' he said, handing her a glass then pouring wine into it.

'You're a very attractive man. You know you are. Shouldn't women be able to act on the same impulses as men?' That sounded convincing. She almost convinced herself.

'Of course they should.'

'Well then . . .' She raised her glass and clinked it against his. Half of her wanted to run away so fast and so far he'd never be able to find her again, while the other half wished she had the courage to ask him to take her straight to bed.

He sipped his wine. 'Let's take it to bed,' he said.

'Fine,' she said, trying to sound calm.

She got to her feet and he led her over to the alcove at the back of the room, putting the bottle and his glass down on one of the bedside tables. He operated a switch on the wall and dark grey blinds rolled out over the skylights. He turned on one of the small bedside lamps and turned off the lights in the rest of the studio.

He was wearing a white shirt, and dark blue slacks, the summer heat making a jacket unnecessary. Without the slightest embarrassment, he unbuttoned his shirt. His broad chest was covered in a thick mat of black hair, his arms shaped by hard, well-defined muscles. His hands, she noticed, were lined with prominent blue veins, the skin sprouting long but sparsely distributed black hairs. They were scrupulously clean, like a doctor's hands, and the fingernails were very regular and looked manicured. His navel was flat with deep hollows on either side carved out by his abdominal muscles. She could see why Angela had been so impressed with the photograph of him stripped to the waist.

He kicked off his shoes and pulled off his black socks, then unzipped his slacks, paying no attention to her, and pulled them down together with his white boxer shorts. His long legs were as muscled as his torso, his thighs, less hairy than his chest, contoured with taut, hard, fibrous tissue. His cock was slightly aroused, protruding from his curly black pubic hair, its circumcised tip as smooth as a billiard ball. The sac of his scrotum was comparatively hairless and hung down heavily between his legs.

Nadia sat on the edge of the bed. Her heart was beating so fast she was sure he would be able to hear it.

Again she realised they hadn't even kissed. The same thought seemed to occur to him. He came to stand in front of her and stooped to kiss her lightly on the lips, holding her cheeks in both his hands.

'You're very lovely,' he said softly. She had never been good at taking compliments but from him the words sounded absolutely sincere.

'Thank you,' she said.

'Would you like me to look the other way?' he said, the contrast between his nudity and her clothes stark.

'No, no . . .' she said, getting to her feet. It was the moment of truth, the point of no return. If she was going to run she would have to run now.

Jack stripped off the counterpane and bedding to leave only the undersheet. He piled the pillows against the wall at the top of the bed and propped himself against them, his legs crossed, his cock and balls sitting on top of his thighs.

With a coolness that surprised her, she pulled the simple white blouse she was wearing out of her skirt and unbuttoned it. She felt perfectly calm and committed. She had got herself into this and now she was determined to go through with it. If she regretted it in the morning, did it really matter? She had had so little to feel anything about recently, even regret would make a pleasant change. And it was possible regret would not be the emotion she would experience.

She unzipped her skirt. It was too tight to fall to the floor of its own accord. She had to wriggle out of it. She tried not to think, keeping her mind in neutral again.

Stepping out of her skirt she picked it up from the floor, only too aware of Hamilton's eyes following her every movement. She folded the skirt over the top of a nearby chair, conscious of the fact that he would be able to see her bottom, the way the white teddy she was wearing had dug itself into the cleft between her buttocks. She thanked some god somewhere that she was wearing decent lingerie, as she stripped her blouse off her shoulders and laid that on the chair too.

She didn't mind him looking at her. She was proud of her body. She wanted him to look. It excited her.

Very deliberately she peeled the thin white shoulder straps of the teddy down over her arms. The lacy cups that held her breasts fell away and she looked at her nakedness. Her nipples were puckered, her tan brown areolae dotted with tiny extrusions like pimples, born of her excitement. There was no doubt what her body wanted.

She pulled the teddy down, over her slim, waspie waist, down over the marked flare of her hips and the tight curves of her buttocks, down until its crotch was inverted, clinging to the plane of her sex as though reluctant to break the intimate contact with her body. With a tug she freed it and the silky white garment fell to the floor.

Her tights were a translucent grey, shiny and sheer. They did not hide the furry triangle below her belly, her short blonde hairs – if he had cared to think about it he would know she was a natural blonde – so neat they looked as though they had been combed to a point, a point that led to the junction of her thighs, like an arrow on the map of her body. She hooked her fingers into the waistband of the nylon.

'No,' he said.

'No?'

'Let me do it for you.'

'If that's what you want.'

'It is.'

She sat on the edge of the bed again and ran her fingers through her short blonde hair, feeling it spring back into place. Her display had swollen his penis. It stood up straight, projecting from the top of his thighs at a right angle. It was big and broad and long, the bulb of his glans like a giant acorn atop a shaft that was veined and rough-cast. As she looked she saw it throb, engorging more. She felt her sex throb too. She was barely in control now. She had succeeded in keeping her mind blank, in pushing

27

reason and good sense aside, to get herself this far but she could no longer control the other side of the equation – her excitement. Doing what she had done had given her a sense of freedom that excited her almost as much as Hamilton had. She felt brave and independent. She couldn't distinguish her intellectual pleasure at what she had done from the strong physical emotions that pounded through her. She wanted this man. She wanted him now. She wanted to feel his hard, muscled body embracing her, wanted those arms wrapped around her, crushing her, wanted that cock, that big throbbing cock, bursting its way into her body, filling her, swamping her, drowning her in the same way she had already drowned in the dark abyss of his eyes.

She turned and ran her hand over his thighs until it brushed his balls. She wanted to take the initiative. His cock pulsed at the touch. She slid her hand down his thigh, caressing it with the lightest of touches. It twitched.

'Do you want me to suck it?' The sound of her voice betrayed her passion.

'Yes,' he said simply.

She knelt up on the bed, the nylon of the tights rasping. Perhaps that was why he hadn't wanted her to take the tights off. Perhaps he had no intention of fucking her; he was just going to lie there and expect her to take him in her mouth.

Sticky fluid had escaped at the tip of his cock, oozing out until it was the shape of a perfect tear, viscous and sticky. Nadine broke it with the very tip of her tongue, pulling back so the string of liquid was spun out, like a spider's web, connecting her lips and his cock. The string finally broke. She dipped again and repeated the process. This time when the connection snapped she plunged her head down on to the hard erect shaft, right the way down until his cock was buried inside her mouth and she closed her lips around its base and felt the curls of his pubic hair against her chin.

Her body churned. His cock was big and hot and so hard, hard like a bone. She sucked on it, sucking it without moving her mouth, feeling her sex throbbing as she imagined – not consciously but reflexively – how it would feel inside her, pressed deep inside her. Reflexively also she flexed her thighs to squeeze her labia together. She could feel the sap of her body spreading out from her loins.

She pulled her mouth back and began a rhythmic motion. He moaned slightly. She did not allow his cock to come all the way out, just to the gate of her lips where her tongue flicked at the slit at its tip, before she plunged down again, all the way down, until his glans nudged right up to the back of her throat. Then she pushed harder, controlling her gagging reflex, as she had learned to do in the past, and feeling his cock jammed hard against the ribbed wall of her windpipe. At the same time she fingered his balls, jiggling them against her chin.

'No,' he said suddenly, his hands gripping her face and pulling her mouth away.

'I thought that's what you wanted,' she teased, feigning innocence.

'You're very good at it . . .'

She was. Another man in her life had wanted nothing else.

'But that's not what I want,' he continued. 'I want to fuck you.' The word 'fuck' sounded different on his lips. It sounded as if it was something she had never done before.

He was pulling her down on to her back while he got up on to his knees. As soon as she settled he leant forward and kissed her lightly on the lips, his mouth just brushing hers, moving from one side to the other, his tongue darting out in little forays to penetrate fleetingly into her moist, hot mouth. Meanwhile the palm of his hand circled her hard nipples, one after the other. He moved his mouth to her neck, sucking and licking and nibbling at her flesh, making her arch her head back against the sheet, stretching the long sinews of her throat so they stood out like cords of rope.

She could hardly believe what was happening to her. She had never felt her body react like this. It was as though she were being strung out, each caress like the ratchet on a mediaeval rack, stretching her further. His mouth followed the taut sinews down to the hollows of her throat, over her collarbone, to the rise of her breast. While his mouth descended, one arm supporting his weight on the far side of her body, the other hand – just the fingertips of the other hand – caressed her belly, drawing imaginary circles with the faintest of touches. She had been caressed like this before but it had never caused her to feel what she was feeling now.

Nadia was on fire, her whole body quivering as his mouth approached her nipple. She could hardly wait for his lips to encircle the swollen, erect cherry that topped her breast. It seemed to be alive, wanting of its own accord, independent of her. Suddenly she felt his hot breath blowing on the puckered flesh and then his mouth sucked it in, not lightly now but hard and fierce, as though trying to encompass the whole breast between his lips, sucking in as much flesh as he could. Releasing everything but the tender puckered nipple, he held it firmly between his teeth. Then he repeated the process with the other breast. The tingle of pain was laced through with the exquisite pleasure.

Nadia's excitement was extreme and she struggled to understand it. Perhaps no more than an hour ago this man had been a total stranger. Now she was lying naked with him, his erection brushing her thigh, his eyes roaming her body. And it was all down to her, her idea, her initiative. She had taken the first step. Was that the cause of her passion? Was it the way she'd abandoned herself? Or was it Hamilton? His body excited her. It was hard and handsome and strong. His touch was perfect too, but she knew it had to be more than that. Her attraction to him was deep. What he was touching was not her body but her mind, stimulating the one part of her sexuality she had never been able to reach before. And the reason he could do that was what she could not understand.

She spread her legs and arched her body off the bed, giving up the attempt to analyse the whys and wherefores. She hoped he would see her need for him, her need to feel his cock plunging into her sex.

'Be patient . . .' he said, reading her perfectly.

His hand ran over her belly. The skin on his hand was rough, like a workman's hand, calloused and hard, and she could hear it rasping against the nylon of her tights. It caressed her thighs, smoothing over the contours of her muscles, down to her knees, then up again on the soft inner surface, until the side of his hand was pressing the nylon against her labia.

He moved his hands to the waistband of the tights and pulled it down over her hips. She co-operated, raising her buttocks from the bed so he could slide the nylon away. He rolled it off her legs one by one then gently opened her legs. She saw him looking at her sex. He was looking at it as she imagined he would look at one of his pictures, admiring, critical, approving, the deckled, wet, scarlet nether lips exposed to his gaze. She felt herself throb powerfully, as if his eyes were touching a raw nerve.

His finger slid into the crease of her labia, her wetness lubricating the movement. He looked into her eyes and she felt herself drowning again. She supposed she had never felt such a physical attraction for a man, uncluttered by social niceties. She had translated the attraction to reality, and now she knew her instinct had been right. She had never responded sexually to any man as she was responding to Hamilton, never, never, never . . .

His finger found her clitoris. She moaned, shaking her head from side to side, as if not able to believe what she was experiencing. Her sex seemed to have come alive, plugged into some source of power that filled it with energy.

Hamilton rocked back on his haunches. He watched her with studied interest as his fingertip brushed her clitoris, the only physical contact between their bodies. It was enough. As he moved the tip against the tiny nut of nerves he saw her arch up off the bed again and knew she was coming. He readied himself, readied himself to spring. He could see her angling herself towards him, almost imperceptibly, her body language artfully expressing her need, her sex open and vulnerable.

Nadia could hardly bear it. Feelings so sharp they were almost painful coursed through her body. His touch was perfect, the perfect pressure, the perfect movement. Men had touched her like this before but never with such finesse or understanding of her needs. It was as though he knew exactly what she wanted because he had complete empathy with what she felt. She managed to open her eyes to look up at him. His mouth was smiling, enjoying her pleasure. She looked down at his single finger moving so tellingly between her legs. It rolled over and around, pushing her clitoris against her pubic bone. Perfect. She felt the tide of orgasm engulf her, her eyes squeezed shut, her body shuddering, her mouth groping to express some sound or other, her nerves and tendons and muscles stretched to the limit.

Before she knew what was happening he had fallen on her like a wolf on its prey, riding up on the flood of her orgasm until his cock was buried so deeply inside her it would have taken her breath away, had she had any breath left. But she did not. She could hardly breathe at all. She was existing on sensation, the purest sensation she had ever experienced, a feeling so tangible, so real it was like a thing apart from her. It was a feeling she knew she would never forget.

She came again instantly, the second his phallus hit the neck of her womb, her whole sex contracting around his big, rock-hard shaft, squeezing it, milking it, the feeling of its strength reinforcing her orgasm, giving it momentum, making it explode higher and longer than she'd ever thought possible. As he moved in her, pumped into her, now with no subtlety or finesse, only hardness and vigour, using

all his considerable power to push deeper than she
could ever remember any man being in her, Nadia
did not know whether she was having one
continuous orgasm or several, so close together
there was no gap between them. All she knew was
she never wanted it to end, and it didn't, not for a
long, long time.

Eventually, though she did not know when, he
must have come too. She would have liked to have
felt him jetting inside her but she was too high, too
overwhelmed, too far gone, too everything, to feel
any more or react any more. She could not move;
she could barely register conscious thought. But she
knew one thing: she had never felt anything like
this before in her life.

When she opened her eyes, he had rolled on to
his side and was looking at her face. There was
something in his eyes she had not expected to see, a
vulnerability, an openness. She saw a little boy's
face, a little boy who had been hurt by life but didn't
like to show it. The aftermath of orgasm had
exposed it, allowed a glimpse behind the face he
presented to the world. Nadia put her arm around
him and cuddled his face to her breast.

The light woke her. Or was it the need to pee? She
had been asleep so deeply that for a moment she
could not remember where she was, let alone what
day it was. As she wrestled herself to consciousness
the facts came flooding back, emotions in Techni-
color, feelings in waves. The light was seeping
through the blinds that covered the skylights.

She looked over at Hamilton. He was lying on his
stomach, his head to one side on the pillow facing
her, his naked body covered by a single sheet that

had been pulled down to his waist. His back was contoured with muscles and his scapulae stuck out prominently. His buttocks, under the sheet, were small and round. His face appeared to be in perfect repose, relaxed and remarkably childlike. She noticed he had black eyelashes so long they looked as though they had been curled with a brush.

Trying not to disturb him, Nadia slipped out of bed and looked around for a bathroom. There was only one internal door and she found a small white tiled shower room behind it, with a shower cubicle, wash-hand basin and toilet. The room had no window and she pulled the cord of the light switch which caused a fluorescent light to flick on with a hum, bathing her in a very white, very shadowless light.

There was a mirror behind the basin and she stared into it. There was no outward sign of last night's activities. Her body revealed no clues as to what she felt. But she felt as though she had been through an emotional wringer, squeezed dry and reconstituted. It seemed to her she *should* look different to match what she felt.

Sitting on the loo she peed long and hard. It was difficult not to think of sex, to start remembering what she had experienced. Immediately her body shuddered. Sex had been a problem in her life for so long, the gnawing inadequacies of her sexual encounters so much part of her personality that it was almost as if she had lost an old friend. Now the idea that she had cultivated and cherished, that some physiological mechanism was missing from her sexual loop, a short circuit in the connection between the erogenous zones and the cybernetics of orgasm, would have to be abandoned. The fact that the orgasms she had experienced before were light years away from what had happened to her last night could only be ascribed to one thing: for the first time in her life she had been with the right man. Even her married man, for all his sophistication, had never made her feel the way Hamilton had done.

She remembered a friend telling her, when she was fifteen and still a virgin, that women only had orgasms when they were truly, madly and deeply in love. She had believed it for a long time. She wondered if it still coloured her life. It was lust, not love that had motivated her actions. Curiously, despite what he had done to her, she did not feel any affection for Jack Hamilton. Knowing herself, however, she knew it would not be long before the spectre of emotional commitment, like an unwelcome ghost, appeared from the shadows.

After washing her hands, Nadia used a piece of toilet paper to wipe away the smudge of make-up under her eyes. She looked at her watch. It was six o'clock. Plenty of time to get home and change before work.

She opened the shower room door and padded naked across the studio floor. One of Hamilton's paintings was on a large wooden easel right under the skylights. It was an odd scene, half a room on one side of the canvas and half a garden on the other, with no dividing line between the two. In the foreground there was an outline of where two figures were obviously to be painted in.

'Morning.'

His voice startled her.

'Hello,' she said, feeling slightly coy about her nakedness.

He was sitting up in bed, smiling sympathetically.

'You found the loo?'

'Yes.' She got back into bed, propped herself up against the pillows and was just about to pull the sheet up over her breasts when some inner voice chided her for being so silly.

Hamilton ran the back of his hand over her cheek.

'You all right?' he asked.

She smiled weakly. 'You know, morning after the night before. I've got to go.'

'Go?'

'Work.'

'Ah, yes. The company that sponsors the gallery. What exactly is it you do there?'

'Actually, I work for a merchant bank.'

'Not just a pretty face. What does it involve? Arranging mergers and takeovers, that sort of thing?'

'That sort of thing exactly. I work in the acquisitions department.' That was definitely a point to him. When she told most men that she worked for a merchant bank they asked her what her boss did, assuming she was an assistant or secretary. It was a long time since Nadia had been either of those. In fact, if her latest venture was successful she would be put on the board and become one of the very few women holding a directorship in a merchant bank.

'Do you want coffee?'

'No, no thanks.'

He was looking at her breasts. Those big, liquid, mahogany eyes were staring at them quite unabashed.

'Do you like them?' she asked, feeling her nipples stiffen under his gaze.

'They're a lovely shape. Your whole body is really

37

exceptional.' He sounded as if he was discussing a painting, an objective assessment that appeared self-evident. Very gently he touched them, one after the other, moulding his fingers to their curves. 'Lovely,' he repeated.

The touch made Nadia's body hum, like a radio turned on but not tuned in.

'I've got to go,' she said weakly, suddenly feeling it was the last thing she wanted to do. She made a quick calculation. A cab to her house would take her thirty minutes, no longer at this time in the morning. She could shower and change and be out of the house in fifteen, and the drive to work was another ten. No more than an hour. It was six now. She didn't need to leave until seven-thirty. She could afford to give in to the impulse that his touch had created.

'I'd like to kiss you,' Hamilton said.

'Why don't you then?'

'I don't want to start anything I can't finish.'

'Oh, I think I've got time for us both to finish,' she said smiling, her pulse beginning to race as her body remembered what he had done to it last night.

He turned towards her and looked straight into her eyes. She felt like a rabbit caught in the headlights of a car, unable to move one way or the other, totally hypnotised. He caressed her cheek again then moved forward until his lips were brushing hers, the heat of his mouth radiating against them.

'Yes,' she whispered, 'oh yes.' The words made her lips move on his. Suddenly he took her by the shoulders, pulled her up towards him and wrapped his arms around her as he plunged his tongue into her mouth and squirmed his lips on hers.

Nadia felt a shock of pleasure. Her body lit up like a Christmas tree, every nerve tingling as if eager to establish that last night had not been a freak and they were capable of operating at the same level of intensity again, of giving and receiving pleasure at this new high frequency. She gasped, the sound gagged on his tongue. She felt her breasts being crushed against his chest, her nipples so hard they felt like pebbles trapped between their bodies.

He was pulling her down on the bed. In seconds he was lying on top of her and she felt his erection throbbing against her belly. He broke the kiss and began to move his mouth down her body, down over the tendons of her neck, stretched taut as her pleasure forced her head back. His lips were hot, planting tiny kisses at regular intervals. He reached her collarbone, then mounted the slope of her right breast. Her nipple throbbed as it felt his mouth approaching. He flicked it with his tongue then pinched it lightly between his teeth. His mouth moved over to her left breast, then gave that nipple the same treatment.

His hand was opening her legs, spreading her thighs apart. His finger nudged into her labia and found her clitoris. It felt swollen and hard. Slowly he began circling it, as his lips sucked on her nipple, coating it with saliva, letting the heat of his mouth engulf it.

'Jack, Jack . . .' she moaned. All the feelings she had experienced last night were back with a vengeance. Her body was energised, able to receive infinite sensation, an instrument that had been tuned up, for the first time, that could respond minutely to the most complex demands of its player. 'You don't know how good that feels.'

'What do you want?' he said.

'Everything, everything . . .'

She felt his finger working relentlessly against her clitoris and his mouth go back to her nipple. Another finger began to play at the gate of her vagina, stretching it and opening it. That was another revelation. She hadn't realised it was so sensitive, so adept at giving pleasure. It felt almost like a second clitoris, or was it just that she was so super-charged with feeling that anywhere he touched would react as though it were a new erogenous zone? She felt her body pulse and knew immediately she was going to come. She groped around with her hand until she found his erection, then grasped it tightly, letting its hardness and size and the memory of how it had been buried in her take her over the top, cresting a wave of pleasure as sharp as any she'd had last night.

He did not stop. His finger continued relentlessly. His mouth worked down over her navel and her body spasmed again as she felt his tongue, hot and wet, replace his finger at exactly the moment the fingers of his other hand, one, two or three fingers, she could not tell, plunged into her sex. She squeezed his cock hard as a response and felt another orgasm breaking through her as effortlessly as the first.

What had he done to her? How had he freed her body, connected up the missing neurons, achieved the ease with which she now mounted the heights she had never got near before? If she'd thought for a moment that last night was some sort of fluke, induced by a mad impulse, her body waking from a coma, only to sink back into unconsciousness again, she knew now it was not. The effect was irreversible.

Energy flowed through her like electricity, powering her pleasure. He was driving his fingers into her in imitation of a cock as his tongue pushed her clitoris up and down. But Nadia wanted more.

'Come here,' she said, pulling his cock in the direction of her mouth so he would know what she meant. Without losing contact with her sex, he swung his thigh over her body and worked back on his knees until his cock was poised above her face.

'Is that what you want?' he said.

'Oh yes.' She pulled his big erection down and took it greedily into her mouth. It was so hard, she could never remember a man feeling so hard, hard like a bone. She snaked her hands around his buttocks as his cock slid into her throat. She felt it pulse. She wondered if she could make him come. She wanted to feel him spattering into her mouth, but she wanted him to come in her sex too. She simply wanted everything.

Nadia tried to concentrate on him, using her mouth as a substitute for her sex, making it cling to him as she sawed it in and out, taking him deep then pulling back until she could see the ridge of the glans at her lips. But it was difficult not to be distracted from her efforts by what he was doing to her. His artful tongue was moving sinuously against her clitoris, making it throb and setting the rest of her nerves on edge. The juices from her sex were so copious his fingers penetrated her effortlessly. As the two feelings coalesced and she felt, again, the first inklings of orgasm, he nudged a finger into the ring of her anus. It was wet from the juices that had run down from her sex. Before she realised what he was doing his finger was pushing forward. There was momentary resistance, then her body opened – not from any conscious signal but reflexively – and he plunged the finger into her rear, up alongside the

41

fingers that already invaded her vagina.

'God . . .' The word was gagged on the spear of flesh she held in her mouth.

She could feel his fingers sliding up and down inside her, the one separated from the others only by the thinnest of membranes, the movement lubricated by a new flood of juices that this extra intrusion had occasioned. Instantly, as he strained the tendons of his finger to get deeper into her, she came. This time her orgasm was like an explosion. It roared through her body with such intensity it was almost painful, the penetration of her vagina as complete as the penetration of her mouth.

Before men had laboured assiduously, even, occasionally, with art and finesse, to pleasure her. She would come, it was true. But not only were the sensations insignificant in comparison with what she was experiencing now, but her orgasm would be singular, her muted climax never to be revived. Now she was multi-orgasmic. She thought she was never going to stop coming. He had found a spot on her clitoris that made her squirm as though it were a button that he only had to push to bring her off. How was it that she had never found it for herself, nor any other man?

She sucked hard on his cock and felt it throb in response. She tried to clear her head, tried to think. Everything was happening so quickly. Suddenly she knew exactly what she wanted. She pulled away from him.

'Let me,' she said.

He raised his head. 'Let you what?'

She squirmed out from under him and came up on her knees. 'It's your turn,' she said, looking into his eyes.

'I've been having my turn.'

'Lie down,' she said. She wanted to show him she wasn't a naive innocent, however much that was what he made her feel. In her struggle to try and get her body to respond she had done what she did with everything else in life – worked hard at it. In business this dedication had brought her success. In sex it had failed – until now. She knew she could make him come for her; she knew what to do.

Hamilton lay on his back. His cock stuck up from his belly, glistening with her saliva. She looked down at him, the muscles of his abdomen as well defined as his biceps and pectorals. The hairs from his chest ran down to form a new pattern on his belly, all pointing inward, thickest in a line right down the centre.

Nadia felt her sex pulse as she looked at his cock. she took it in her hand, curling her fist around it so the glans stuck up above the ring of her thumb and forefingers. With her other hand she traced a finger over the smooth glans. The whole shaft reacted by spasming in her hand.

'God, I want you,' she said almost to herself.

Without letting go of his erection she swung her thigh over his navel and sat up on her haunches, poised above him. He was looking at her like an indulgent father prepared to put up with the antics of his child.

'You're very hard,' she said.

'You make me hard. You're a very sexy woman.'

'Am I?' Oddly she couldn't remember any man ever using that adjective about her before. She was used to 'lovely', 'beautiful', even 'gorgeous'. But not 'sexy'. She guided his cock between her legs and used it to open her labia. Her juices anointed it.

'You know you are.'

43

She sunk down on him, her thighs spread open, his cock plunging into her vagina, his pubic bone grinding against her clitoris. He filled her. He was so deep she could feel his glans touching the neck of her womb just as, minutes before, it had been forced down her throat. With all her energy she concentrated on squeezing him with her sex.

'Very strong,' he said, laughing.

She liked that. She laughed too. His laughter intoxicated her. She had never laughed in bed before. It had all been too dour and serious. Now she was relaxed and confident.

'I'm going to make you come.' She emphasised the word 'make'.

'Are you?'

'You want to come, don't you, come inside me?' The words made her whole body shudder.

'Yes.'

'Do it then.'

She began to ride up and down on him, sliding his cock in and out, squeezing it with her internal muscles, grinding her clitoris down on him. She took her breasts in her hands as the movement was making them slap against her chest. She played with her nipples and hoped he could feel the tremor this produced in her nerves. Releasing one breast she reached behind her back and captured the sac of his balls.

'Love that,' he said as he felt her fingers reeling it in.

She grasped it tightly, squeezing his balls firmly but gently. 'Like this?'

'You'll make me come.'

'That's what I want.'

'What about you?'

'Come for me.' Didn't he realise she'd come already more than she could ever remember coming in her life?

She jiggled his balls in her hand and felt his cock react. He reached out and held her by the hips, forcing her down on him and preventing her moving up again. He squirmed underneath her, forcing his cock from side to side, then stopped. He had found his place. Sure now that she understood she did not need to move, he put his hands on her breasts, caressing them with such tenderness, feeling their weight and shape, moving his fingers against the nipples, that Nadia's body trembled.

'So good,' she muttered.

'Yes it is.' And with that his cock jerked inside her, once, then twice, then in a continuous spasm as his hot semen jetted into the wet, silky caches of her sex.

From being in control, from wanting pleasure only for him, Nadia felt her body leap. She had never felt ejaculation so graphically, every inch of his erection touching her, every nerve of her sex so sensitised she was sure she could feel the semen spattering inside her. In her mind's eye she could see it, the jets cascading out from the little eye at the end of his cock, white semen washing down the walls of her sex. The image provoked her as much as the fact. A pulse of feeling, like a shock wave, flowed over her, cancelling everything but the sensation of hardness and power buried in the depths of her, depths it had turned to sticky liquefaction.

Chapter Three

'*PHONE CALL FOR* you, says it's personal,' Nadia's secretary told her.

'Thanks.' Nadia heard the click as the call was put through. 'Hello?'

'Nadia. It's Margaret.'

'Margaret, how are you?' Nadia had expected it to be Hamilton. Then she realised why Margaret was calling. 'Is there any news?'

'She's dead, Nadia. Died a month ago.'

'Definitely Nora Babcock?'

'Definitely Nora Babcock. They had a quiet funeral at Marie Ste-Eglise.'

'I bet it was quiet. Margaret, I owe you a big one.'

'Don't be silly, Nadia.'

'No, I do. I'll come over and ski in the winter and make proper recompense.'

'You don't need to do a thing. We're old friends.'

They chatted a while about the weather in Switzerland, where Margaret was calling from, but Nadia's mind wasn't really on the conversation. She was too busy thinking about the implications of what she had learnt. Eventually they said their

46

goodbyes. Nadia found herself grinning broadly.

'What are you doing here?' The office door had opened as she'd put the phone down.'

Angela Barrett grinned as she stood in the doorway. She was wearing a dark green suit, the skirt of which was not much longer than the jacket. Her long legs were sheathed in very sheer, almost transparent nylon.

'As I was passing I thought I'd buy you lunch.'

Nadia was just about to protest that she didn't have time for lunch when Angela produced two paper bags from behind her back. 'Smoked salmon and cream cheese,' she said. 'And a half bottle of Chablis.'

She set the packets down on Nadia's large rosewood desk and fetched two cups from the credenza behind the door where a coffee-making machine was perched. A bottle opener was produced from her handbag.

'I had to see Travers at two so I thought . . .'

'What's Travers up to?' Nadia asked.

'He's looking for another acquisition apparently.'

'He's only just finished the last.'

'This one's much bigger. And the banks think he's the best thing since high fibre bread.'

'He's got the money?' Nadia was astonished.

'Every penny.' Angela unwrapped a sandwich from its cling film and passed it over to Nadia together with a cup of Chablis. 'Cheers,' she said, raising her cup. 'So how did you get on last night.'

'Fine,' Nadia said, trying to sound noncommittal. For once she didn't want to rush into telling Angela everything that had happened.

'Good pictures?'

'I'd seen them already at the preview. I think he's

very talented.' Oh yes, very talented, she said to herself, trying not to let the smug grin she felt on the inside spread to her face. 'There were a couple that are really moving. You should go.'

'Sounds interesting.'

'If I pull this deal off with Anderson I may buy one.' She hadn't thought about that until this minute but it was true. She would like the one she'd seen in the studio. It would remind her of what had happened, as if she needed any reminder.

'And did you meet the great man?'

'He was there.' Nadia hoped her voice didn't betray her.

'Gorgeous, isn't he?'

'He was OK.'

'Oh come on. Don't tell me you didn't find him attractive.'

'Yes, he was attractive.' Nadia tried not to give anything away but felt herself squirming unconsciously against the chair. She had a vivid image of Hamilton lying on the bed, his cock gripped firmly in her fist.

'Did you actually meet him?'

Nadia bit into her sandwich. It tasted delicious, slightly salty with the added smoothness of cream cheese. She felt her sex pulse. It didn't taste dissimilar from Hamilton's cock. 'Yes,' she said when she'd finished chewing. She sipped the Chablis.

'And his wife?'

The word made Nadia go cold. She felt a rush of adrenaline as though she had been startled awake from a deep sleep. She tried to put the cup down on her desk without making Angela aware that her hand had started to shake.

'His wife?' she said in a voice that was far from level.

'She's supposed to be a real beauty. Long black hair. You must have seen her. She's the face of Pandora.'

Pandora was a range of cosmetics that advertised heavily in magazines and on billboards, using the same model's face in all their photographs. Nadia passed one on the way to work, and could see the woman's face immediately. She was beautiful with long hair parted down the middle, her cheekbones high and hollow, her rather thin lips always pictured without the trace of a smile, her big dark eyes perfectly served by the company's products.

'Her? She's married to Jack?'

'Didn't you know?'

'I didn't know anything about him except what you told me the other day. Why didn't you tell me he was married?' The question came out all wrong: too much emphasis and too emotionally charged.

'Why are you so interested suddenly?' Angela said, picking up on her tone. They had been friends for too long for it to pass unnoticed.

It was no time to lie. 'Because I was with him last night, damn him. Damn him to hell.' A thought occurred to her. 'That's why he took me to his bloody studio.'

'You went to bed with him? You sly dog. Why didn't you tell me? You went to bed with Jack Hamilton. What was it like? Was it wonderful? God, I bet it was. I'm green . . .'

'Stop it, Angela. He didn't tell me he was married.'

'Oh Nadia, what does it matter? You had a good time, didn't you?'

49

'You know how I feel about married men.' The spectre of what had happened to her before loomed large. She had sworn she was never going to allow herself to be hurt that way again. Now, unwittingly, she had already committed the crime. The tingling that Hamilton's name had created in her body turned to hard-edged ice.

'Oh come on, Nadia . . .'

'And he lied to me.'

'Did he tell you he wasn't married?'

'No, but . . .'

'He probably assumed you knew. It's common knowledge.'

'Well, I didn't. I'd never have gone to bed with him if . . .' Suddenly she wondered if that was true. She remembered the strength of the impulse she'd felt when she first saw him.

'So he took you to his studio, and . . .?'

'Yes, presumably he takes all his bimbos there. Fully equipped. Double bed. Shower room. Kitchen. I even got freshly brewed coffee.'

'Why are you so cross?'

'I'm not like you, Angela, you know that. I find it difficult to be casual about sex.' Particularly wonderful, mind-bending, earth-shattering sex, she thought but did not say. 'And you know what happened with Jeffrey Allen.'

'I know, I know you were hurt.' She leant forward over the desk. 'But what was he like?' She almost whispered.

'Oh Angela, that's the trouble. That's the *real* problem.'

'What?'

'It was fantastic. I mean, like nothing I've ever experienced before, damn him.'

50

He'd got up after they'd made love, pulled on a short cotton robe and gone to the kitchen. He'd made a pot of coffee in a cafetière and squeezed her a glass of fresh orange juice in an electric juicer. He'd brought it to bed on a white tray. She had ten minutes before her seven-thirty deadline. He touched her face and looked at her in that way he had, as though he were looking at some peerless work of art. She had not recovered from their sex. Her nipples were still so hard she was beginning to think they would never go down and her clitoris seemed to be alive, pulsating constantly against her labia. She felt a sense of well-being that seemed to radiate from her like light from a lighthouse.

He'd told her to get dressed. As he watched her climb into her skirt and blouse he said she had a beautiful body and when she'd looked round again he was erect, his cock poking out from the folds of the robe, as he stroked it gently.

'See what you do to me?' he said.

The desire to take him again, to pull him down on top of her, was almost irresistible. But he could see what was going on in her mind.

'No,' he'd said firmly. 'Go to work. You said you've got to go to work.'

'I have,' she'd agreed. 'But I could . . .' She had *never* considered missing work before.

'No. If you do something you'll regret later then you'll associate that with me. It'll be my fault. I don't want to be associated in your mind with anything but pleasure. Sheer unadulterated pleasure.'

It was exactly what she'd wanted to hear because it implied they had a future.

'Will I see you again?'

'Of course. Don't be ridiculous. Give me your

51

number. I'll call you. As you can see, I can hardly wait.' His erection was testimony to that.

She'd driven home on a high. She'd been on a high ever since. She'd see him again, have sex with him again. Over and over again. She knew she'd never be satiated, not on what he made her feel.

'Christ, Angela,' she said, feeling betrayed. The tears started to well in her eyes but she fought them back. She wasn't going to let that bastard make her cry. 'What am I supposed to do now?'

'How did you leave it with him?'

'Oh, he was terrific. Took my number. Swore he'd call me. Said he couldn't wait. All that crap.'

'I'm sure he'll call.'

'So am I. Positive. Why wouldn't he? You're right. He'll have assumed I knew he was married.' She opened the drawers of her desk one after the other until she found what she wanted. The brochure from the exhibition was in the bottom drawer. She flicked to the back page where Hamilton's photograph stared back at her. The biographical notes ended with the fact that he was married to model Jan Hamilton. 'It's even in here. So he thinks I'm a willing accomplice. A nice juicy bit on the side, one in a very long line.'

'So? Come on, Nadia. What difference does it make? You say you had a good time. You're both adults.'

'No. He's married, Angela.'

'It's not going to be like Jeff. Just have a fling. As you say, there's probably been a whole netball team before you. I'd do it at the drop of a paintbrush.'

'Do what?'

'Go to bed with Jack Hamilton.' Angela took a large bite from her sandwich.

Nadia had lost her appetite. She felt angry and used. The night with Hamilton had been so special, she'd found it impossible to put him out of her thoughts all morning. It was not that she had become emotionally involved with him – though she knew in time that would have been inevitable. But she was physically involved and that was much worse. She had developed an instant obsession, an addiction, and weaning herself away from it was going to be hard.

'Got to go,' Angela said. 'Aren't you going to eat that?' She was looking at the half-eaten sandwich.

'No.'

'Don't mind if I do?' she said, reaching across the desk. She finished the sandwich in two big bites. All Angela's appetites were voracious.

'Thanks for the wine.'

'You in tonight? I'll call you.'

'No, I've got dinner at the Dorchester. Dick Cabot, that Canadian on the board of Tresko. He wants to sell.'

'Really?'

'I've placed the whole lot at quite a premium. The shares will jump.'

'I didn't hear that,' Angela said.

'I didn't say it.'

Angela waved and was gone, leaving Nadia staring at the files on her desk, her enthusiasm for work, as for everything else, suddenly flown out of the window.

It was twelve o'clock when Dick Cabot finally refused an offer of Hine Antique. Up to that point he had accepted gladly and often, and the bill, which Angela paid, was commensurately large. He appeared little the worse for wear, however, and courteously allowed Nadia to take the first taxi the doorman whistled up.

'It's good work,' he told her as she climbed aboard.

'I'll put it all in a fax tomorrow.'

'Great. Send it to Toronto. I'm leaving in the morning.'

It had been a good evening's work. The fact that she had been able to place the shares at such a good premium to the market price had so impressed Cabot that he had told her he would undoubtedly use her for his next major UK deal, which, though he would give no details, was already being planned.

But as the taxi wound its way along a deserted Oxford Street, Nadia could find no consolation in her business acumen. The spectre of Jack Hamilton continued to haunt her. She could see his face, the way those mahogany eyes had looked at her with such intensity, and his strong, naked body. She could see the way his laughter had wrinkled his face and the way he had looked at her as she'd sunk her sex down on to his erection. She could see every detail of his cock, its veins and contours like an animate relief map of her pleasure. She shuddered and, with an effort, tore her mind away from the taunting images.

'Damn you,' she said aloud.

'Sorry, miss?' the taxi driver said, thinking she was talking to him.

'Nothing. Talking to myself.'

'That's a bad habit, miss.'

'I know.'

Outside her house she gave the driver a big tip.

He didn't drive away until she was opening the front door, a gesture of consideration she appreciated. After turning off her burglar alarm she went straight up to her bedroom, stripped off the red silk dress she had been wearing and ran herself a bath. She needed to try and relax. She felt like the mainspring of a watch that had been wound too tight.

She lay in the bath and tried to concentrate on what she had to do the next day. A major takeover bid was due to be announced by the middle of the following week. Her clients had tried to negotiate with the company they wanted to buy, Anderson Aggregates, but all reasonable offers had been refused. They had decided to launch a bid which naturally Anderson's would oppose. There was going to be a major battle with the big institutional shareholders on both sides holding all the cards. But Nadia had developed another strategy. It depended on her getting to see Andrew Anderson in person and, as she was firmly in the enemy camp, there would certainly be no way he would agree to that on a formal basis. But the next day she was meeting a man who knew Anderson well and who had offered to introduce her casually, as if by chance. Then she would be able to see if the information her friend Margaret had given her that morning would be as valuable as she thought it was.

Drying herself quickly she walked back into the bedroom and got into bed. It had been a pleasantly warm night and Nadia had no need for more than a single sheet to cover her. She picked up her book from the bedside table and read a page or two. She caught a glimpse of herself in the mirror opposite the bed, the outline of her naked body – she always slept in the nude – under the peach-coloured sheet. It reminded her of Angela's story. She felt her nipples stiffen. She could see them clearly cresting the firm hills of her breasts. She opened her legs, creating a V-shaped valley, the sheet clinging to the roundness of her thighs.

And then it was too late. Too late to control herself, too late to do anything but plunge her hand down over the delta of her pubis, her fingers curving round the bone into the softness of her labia. She threw the book aside, her hand rigid against her sex. In the mirror she saw her middle finger move, crooking inward to find her clitoris, rubbing against the sheet.

'Damn you,' she said aloud. It had become her litany.

She pulled the sheet off her body, bent her knees with her legs wide apart and lifted her buttocks, staring into the open mouth of her own sex. Why was she lying here alone? Why wasn't she with him? She wanted to feel that big, incredibly hard cock throbbing in her hand. She wanted to suck it. She wanted it inside her.

With one hand she held her right breast, squeezing it tightly, while the other went back to her sex. Her body seemed to be mocking her, throbbing with the same anticipation she had felt with Hamilton. But she knew it would be useless. She would achieve nothing from masturbation but disappointment and anti-climax. Half of her didn't even want to try, just wished she could roll over and sleep. The other half sent her hand down over her belly, her finger parting her labia to find the promontory of her clit. To her surprise she was wet. Not just moist but soaking wet. She had never felt herself like this under these circumstances. She moved her fingers down to the gate of her vagina. Her whole sex was liquid. It felt different too, like a squashy, over-ripe fruit. She felt it throb at her touch, a surge of feeling so strong it made her gasp.

Of course, she was seeing Hamilton now. She could see him in the mirror standing by the bed, quite naked, his erection sticking out at a right angle from his body. He was looking down at her, with an indulgent expression on his face.

'Watch me, then,' she said aloud, opening her legs wider, arching her body up at the imaginary image, showing herself to him. 'Watch me.'

She plunged two fingers into her sex, pushing them in until the tendons of her hand were strained to the limit. But it wasn't deep enough. Her mind wanted the feeling of Hamilton's cock driving up to the neck of her womb. The odd thing was that she had never penetrated herself like this before. Occasionally she would put a finger into her sex but it had never excited her very much. Not like this. Now she wanted penetration. She needed something inside her, and needed it desperately.

Nadia looked around the room for some phallic object to serve as a substitute for Hamilton's presence. She had a small set of exercise weights stacked in a corner. The central spindle of the dumbbells could be disconnected to add extra weight. It was made from some sort of plastic and, apart from the ridges where the circular weights could be fitted, was perfectly smooth. She leapt off the bed, pulled the weighted ends off the spindle and carried it back to bed, resuming her position with her knees bent and her legs open. Her sex was throbbing. Her imagination made the spindle throb in her hand too.

She looked into the mirror. She touched the end of the spindle to her nipple, imagining it was Hamilton's cock. She pressed it down into the spongy flesh. The plastic was cold to the touch and made her nipples pucker even tighter.

Hamilton was looking at her again. He'd taken his cock in his hand as if to say, 'Wouldn't you rather have this?'

'No,' she said in answer to the unasked question. 'I don't need you.'

She trailed the phallus down over her belly. She wasn't seriously going to stick this thing inside her, was she? She'd never put any foreign object inside her vagina. But she needed it. She desperately needed to feel something hard and strong filling her, mimicking, however inadequately, the feeling Hamilton's cock had given her.

The end of the phallus nudged into her labia. She felt it butt against her clitoris, and used it to circle the little nut of nerves. She imagined she had Hamilton's cock in her hand and was manipulating his glans against her.

'Feels so good, doesn't it?'

Her masturbation had always been silent before. Now the words excited her. She moved the phallus down between her legs, her own juices lubricating its journey. She couldn't believe what she was feeling, the excitement that was coursing through her body.

'Come on then, put into me,' she said for her own benefit. 'Fuck me.'

She could see every detail of his cock. She could feel everything he had done to her, how his fingers had plunged into both passages of her body, how his tongue had licked at her sex, how his erection had overwhelmed her. With no hesitation she drove the spindle into her body. She was so wet it slid up effortlessly, until the end was deep inside her. The initial penetration produced a wave of feeling so strong it forced her eyes closed. She dropped her head back on the pillow. She imagined him looking down at her. Her sex contracted involuntarily, gripping the phallus as if to test its solidity.

'Yes, yes, like that,' she cried, forcing the phallus deeper.

And then the strangest thing happened, strange for her at least. She came. She came easily, with no exertion, no desperation, no prolonged, increasingly anguished striving. She came like she'd never come before by her own hand, a sharp, powerful orgasm that gathered in all her feelings and emotions and put them to work to pleasure her completely.

Her surprise was absolute. As soon as she could react consciously again she opened her eyes and looked into the mirror, seeing the astonishment written all over her face.

'Did you see that?' she asked her imaginary lover.

She was not finished. She knew that. She moved the phallus up and down. Her body was going to give her more. She could feel every contour of the object inside her. She could feel the silky wet walls of her vagina as it moved against them. As if to attract her attention her clitoris pulsed strongly. Holding the phallus in one hand she moved the other over her belly. Even the fur of her pubic hair seemed to be alive with feeling. She pushed her finger down into her labia. The breadth of the spindle had opened them and her clitoris was already exposed. It was swollen and incredibly tender. She stroked it gently and felt a surge of sensation course through her. It flashed down to her vagina and broke over the end of the phallus, causing another contraction.

'Fuck me then,' she said. 'Come on, fuck me.'

It was all so different. The words were provoking her. So was everything she could see in the mirror, the end of the phallus sticking out obscenely from the soft folds of her labia, the rest of it buried in her sex. She pushed the phallus in and out, imitating the action of a cock, of his cock, Hamilton's cock. The plastic had taken the warmth of her body. It had seemed to be alive. It was not difficult to imagine it was *him*.

She wished she could pinch her nipples. She wished she could push a finger into her rear passage. She wanted everything all at once. But this was enough. More than enough. She matched the rhythm of the penetration with the movements of her finger on her clitoris, suddenly adept and fluent, for the first time, at the rites of masturbation. She pushed her clitoris from side to side against the hardness of her pubic bone. Her whole body was alive, like it had been with Hamilton, so alive, so full of excitement, she found it hard to believe it had not responded like this before.

An orgasm flooded over her, sweeping everything aside but the intensity of pleasure. Almost immediately, as she continued to plunge the dildo to and fro, another began, this time swelling like a wave at the beach, gathering momentum, until it crashed over her, knocking her back into an undertow of sensation. She was writhing on the bed, tossing her head from side to side, her breasts slapping against each other. It was a storm, a cyclone of feeling.

60

Eventually the crisis passed. She could not take any more. She eased the spindle out of her body and looked at it curiously. It was glistening with her juices. Her labia and her clitoris felt a little sore, which was not surprising. She had been out of control and had hammered them mercilessly. But, as she looked into the mirror, she saw she was grinning.

She got off the bed a little unsteadily and went into the bathroom to pee. Her body was completely relaxed now, the mainspring wound down. She felt wonderful, little trills and remembrances of pleasure still occasionally jolting through her. Sex, she thought, must be like riding a bicycle. Once you learnt to do it you never forgot how. She laughed out loud. She had obviously never been taught properly before. She had assumed that whatever neural pathways Hamilton had opened would close again without his endeavours. She was delighted to find the effect he had had on them appeared to be permanent.

Getting back into bed she covered herself with the sheet. The touch of the cotton against her nipples gave her a tingling sensation. They felt incredibly sensitive. Her sex too reacted to the pressure of her thighs as she brought her legs together. She had gone from the sublime to the ridiculous, from the ice maiden to the fire queen. She was even tempted to touch herself again, exactly like a child with a new toy, who wanted to play with it, just one more time before bed.

The image of Hamilton hadn't faded. He was still there if she looked up into the mirror, his body turned sideways so she could see the projection of his cock jutting out from his belly, its curved shaft and the sac of his balls like some exotic fruit ripe to be picked. But, for all her passion, she was still furious with him for what he'd done.

The trouble was, it was probably too late to protect herself against him. Hamilton had already touched her in a way no other man had. He had reached into her libido and found the key to her sexuality. He had let the genie out of the lamp and now it roamed free, gaining strength and power and wanting to enjoy its new-found capabilities. It was difficult to stay cross with him. She saw his smile, and the warmth in his eyes . . .

'Damn you,' she said, chanting her litany. Why did he have to be married?

Chapter Four

ANGELA ANSWERED ON the second ring. 'Hello?'

'Hi, it's me. What are you doing?'

'Finishing up.'

'Do you feel like going out tonight?'

'Great. What time?'

'The Rencontre at seven-thirty.'

'The Rencontre? What's got into you?' Rencontre was in Berkeley Square. It was a bar and restaurant and was usually packed with women hunting in pairs among the prosperous male clientele. Women were allowed in free; men had to pay an exorbitant membership fee.

'You know exactly,' Nadia said pointedly.

'Oh right. Withdrawal symptoms.' Angela laughed.

'Get dressed up. I'm going to.'

'If that's what you want.'

'See you later.'

He had called her three times. Each time she had told her secretary to tell him she wasn't available. Each time the temptation to push the button on her phone that would put him through was almost irresistible. But she had resisted, just. She badly needed to take her mind, and her body, off him.

Two hours later Nadia sat on one of the barstools at the far end of the long bar of Rencontre, toying with a glass of champagne, and aware of the many pairs of eyes that roamed her body. She was wearing a black Ferragamo dress that clung to her figure. Its plunging neckline revealed the depth of her cleavage and a split in its skirt exposed a great deal of thigh. She wore a silver choker around her neck and had made herself up with less subtlety than usual: a heavy eye shadow to emphasise her eyes, a blusher to accentuate her cheekbones and a dark red lipstick to match the colour of her fingernails. She had sheathed her legs in sheer black tights that were woven with Lycra to give them a glossy finish and was wearing her highest high heels. She crossed her legs and let the split in the skirt reveal her thigh. It was an uncharacteristic gesture for her but oddly she found it exciting. She watched one man in a booth opposite staring fixedly. He was in his fifties with a bald pate and teeth yellowed by smoking. He was trying to catch her eye but she refused to play *that* game.

'Darling!' Angela exploded into the bar through the swing doors at the far end and pushed her way through the crowd. She kissed Nadia on both cheeks. 'Sorry I'm late, got a phone call just as I was leaving.'

'Don't worry.' Nadia signalled to the barman to bring two glasses of champagne without asking Angela what she wanted.

Angela squirmed on to the barstool Nadia had kept vacant for her. She was wearing a cobalt-blue dress that looked as though it had been sprayed on, no more than a tight tube of material clinging to her body from the top of her breasts to the middle of her thighs. On the front, over her navel, it was decorated with a figure of eight picked out in silver sequins. Her red hair had been pinned up to her head, rather severely emphasising her long neck and the bareness of her shoulders. Like Nadia she also wore Lycra tights but hers were patterned with a diamond motif. The blue of her high heels matched her dress. They had straps from the back of the heel around her narrow ankles.

'Have you sized up the talent?' Angela asked, blatantly looking at the ranks of men sitting opposite, only a very few as yet attached to female companions.

'Not really.'

The barman put the glasses of champagne on the bar in front of them. Nadia used the rest of her first glass to make the libation.

'So tell Auntie Angela all about it.' Angela had known her friend too long not to know what lay behind a visit to Rencontre, dressed up like a dog's dinner.

'It's Hamilton. I can't get him out of my mind.'

'He must have been good.'

'Can I ask you something really personal?' Nadia leant closer to her friend.

'Of course.'

'Do you use a dildo?' She didn't have to ask whether Angela masturbated. She knew she did. Angela had told her some time ago that she masturbated regularly, often as much as two or three times a week. She needed it, she had told Nadia, even if she had been having sex with a man. But the revelation had not included questions of technique.

'A dildo?' Angela repeated. The barman was hovering and smiled broadly but said nothing.

'You know . . .' Nadia tried to think of another word to describe it.

'You mean a vibrator . . . yes, of course I use a vibrator. They're wonderful. Don't you?'

'I . . .' Nadia faltered, suddenly wishing she hadn't brought up the subject. She took a sip of the champagne and lowered her voice, since the barman was clearly hoping he might hear further tit-bits of their conversation. 'No, I hadn't before.'

'What, you've just tried one?'

'I don't know what's happening to me, Angela. I'm just horny all the time. I never used to be like that.' Nadia had made a decision. She had to lay the ghost of Hamilton. She needed a man. She needed to find a man and sleep with him. That was why she'd invited Angela. She didn't have the courage to do it alone, but with Angela along it would be easy. Well, easier.

'And this is all down to Hamilton.'

'Yes.' She wanted to tell her everything.

'Angela, my dear girl . . .' A small, neat man in his late fifties had come up behind them. He had a prolific growth of totally white hair which years of combing in the same direction had laid into a set pattern and small green eyes that sparkled with devilment. His white moustache was slightly turned up at the ends. He wore a tweed suit, and despite the summer temperatures, a yellow camel-haired waistcoat. His Viyella shirt did not match his MCC tie.

'Georgie!' Without getting off the barstool Angela kissed him on both cheeks. His arm snaked around her back and stayed there. 'This is Nadia Irving,'

Angela said. 'Sir George Pontsonby.'

'Charmed,' he said, taking Nadia's hand and bringing it to his lips. 'And this is my nephew, Tony.'

A tall young man stood uneasily behind Sir George. He looked as though he found the décolleté dresses of both women embarrassing and wasn't sure whether he was supposed to look at them. Inevitably his eyes strayed downwards and came to rest on their bosoms.

'Hello, Tony,' Angela said, extending her hand. 'This is Nadia.'

'I'm very pleased to meet you,' he said earnestly, blushing a light shade of pink as he shook their hands in turn. He was no more than nineteen and wore a smart navy blue suit and a white silk shirt with a blue silk tie.

'Georgie and I met at the polo at Cowdray Park,' Angela told Nadia.

'Bloody awful game,' Sir George said immediately. 'Anything that involves horses involves shit and anything that involves shit is shitty.' His remark made him laugh. Angela laughed too. Tony and Nadia merely smiled politely.

'Why did you go then?' Nadia asked.

'Some damn Jap wanted to see it. Angie was the only compensation.'

'George is in property finance,' Angela explained.

'Trying to sell Buckinghamshire to the Nips. Not very sporting. But we all have to earn a crust.'

'And what do you do?' Nadia asked Tony, his attention having fallen to her nylon-covered thigh.

'Oh . . . oh . . .' He blushed again, caught in the act. 'I'm reading Greats at Cambridge.'

'Greats?' Angela queried.

'Classics.'

'Romans and Greeks,' Sir George explained. 'Best possible education for a man. I tell you, this country went to the dogs when civil servants weren't obliged to have Greats from Oxbridge. Essential. Teaches you everything. So are you on?'

'On?' Angela asked.

'On. For the evening. Car's outside. Got a table booked at Le Dernier Cri. Are you game?'

'Georgie, you can't take us there.'

'Can,' he said like a petulant schoolboy. 'Shall.'

'What is it?' Nadia asked.

'A private club with a very risqué cabaret,' Angela said.

'*Le plus risqué*,' Sir George added. 'Come on, dear ladies, no time to waste. The food is superb.'

'Well?' Angela asked Nadia.

'Why not?' Nadia said, putting aside her initial reluctance as she looked at Tony. He was undoubtedly attractive. His hair was blond and his eyes a deep, almost turquoise blue. He had a square set jaw, a fleshy mouth and a very clear complexion that looked as though he got a lot of fresh air, probably playing contact sports. He might be exactly what she was looking for.

'Right,' Sir George exclaimed, extracting a fifty pound note from his pocket and waving it at the barman to pay for the women's drinks. He helped them off the barstools and ushered them out before the barman could return with his change.

Good chauffeurs seem to have a second sense when it comes to knowing when they are required and, as the doorman at the club opened the outer doors for them, a Rolls Royce Silver Wraith glided up to the curb. A slender black chauffeur rushed round to open the nearside passenger door. He was wearing a grey uniform with a crossover front to its jacket and riding breeches for trousers. His black boots were spotless.

'I'll ride up front,' Sir George said as the two women sandwiched Tony between them on the rear seat.

As the car pulled away the glass partition that divided the passengers from the driver slid down and Sir George turned round, hooking his arm over the back of the seat.

'Did I tell you that you're looking particularly stunning, my dear? Stunning. Well, you both do. Don't they, Tony?'

'Lovely,' Tony agreed, only too aware of the two women sitting with elegantly crossed legs on either side of him.

'So what do you do, my dear?' Sir George asked Nadia.

'I work for Hill Brothers.'

'Oh jolly good. Like to see it myself. Women are a bloody underused resource in this benighted country.'

The Rolls halted in a small mews off Curzon Street. It was dimly lit with no functioning street lights and looked like a wholly residential mews with no sign of commercial activity, except for a discreet brass plate on the one building that was a good size bigger than the rest. The plate read: LE DERNIER CRI. PRIVATE MEMBERS ONLY.

As the black chauffeur let them out of the car the club door opened, no doubt alerted to their presence by the security camera mounted in the corner of the small forecourt in front of the house. A huge man filled the doorway. He was wearing a dinner suit and black bow tie, his shoulders so wide he would not have been able to get through the door without turning sideways. Incongruously he wore a small bowler hat.

'Good evening, Archibald,' Sir George said.

'Evening, sir.' The man's voice was falsetto. He stood aside to let them enter, closing and bolting the door behind them.

They found themselves in a small square foyer tastefully decorated with pale pink walls and red carpet. A large oil which Nadia thought was possibly a Pissarro dominated one wall. There was a single oak-panelled door behind a leather-topped Victorian partner's desk.

'Good evening, Sir George.' An attractive auburn-haired woman in a dinner jacket, white silk shirt and black bow tie sat behind the desk. She wasn't wearing trousers or a skirt and Nadia could see the 'shirt' was, in fact, a body worn over black fishnet tights. She typed Sir George's name into the computer that was perched on the desk. 'Three guests, sir.'

'Correct.'

'Very good, sir.'

The panelled door opened and a tall, long-legged, long-haired blonde held it open. She was wearing shiny, almost transparent tights and a leotard made from a fabric that glistened under the light and was coloured to look like silver. It was cut so high on the hip its crotch was no more than a thin thong of material barely covering the crease of her sex. The woman's breasts were large and they bulged out of the plunging neckline of the garment.

'Evening, Sir George,' she said, confirming the impression that he was a respected regular at the club.

70

They filed through the door and were led along a short corridor into a large room. To all intents and purposes it looked like a normal restaurant. There was a small bar area by the entrance which opened into a large space set with tables, glittering with crystal glasses and silver cutlery on pink table cloths. A huge display of flowers, mostly of arum lilies, stood on a table against one wall, individually lit by a spotlight overhead.

Beyond the tables was a dance floor and beyond that a small stage. A trio of musicians sat on the stage playing jazz versions of standard ballads. At the moment they were playing a version of 'Misty', the drummer and bass player providing a muted accompaniment to the skilful improvisation of the pianist.

'Have a nice evening,' the blonde said, making the twenty-pound note Sir George palmed into her hand disappear, as if by magic.

'Can I get you a drink before dinner?' A waitress had come over as they settled into the armchairs in the bar. She was wearing an identical outfit to the blonde's, except the colouring was gold. Sitting down Nadia found herself staring up into the girl's barely covered crotch. One thing was certain. The bikini line treatment for these outfits required complete depilation.

They drank champagne and ordered an extravagant dinner, urged on by Sir George. They were moved to a table in the restaurant where they feasted off oysters and fillet steak and vanilla soufflés, and drank Perrier-Jouet champagne and Romanée-Conti burgundy.

'My attitude,' Sir George declared during the meal, 'is that you should always have the best you can afford.'

The restaurant was busy. There were several Arab customers – men with swarthy complexions, silk suits in pale colours with lapels and facings edged with satin, and tieless shirts, their fingers beringed with gold, their wrists weighed down with elaborate watches, some encrusted with diamonds. The women that accompanied them were all European, all extremely attractive, and all wearing evening dresses in satin or silk or lace, tightly sheathing their bodies while giving tantalising glimpses of breast or thigh.

The maître d' was a woman, though she was dressed in a very masculine dinner suit, with her hair cut and parted exactly like a man. In fact, Nadia had noticed, the entire staff of the club, apart from the bouncer outside, were women. As they finished their meal and were served coffee the maître d' stepped across the dance floor, mounted the small stage and took a microphone from its stand.

'And now, ladies and gentlemen . . .' she said, turning to the audience. 'Le Dernier Cri is proud to present for your entertainment this evening the singular talents of Madame Morceau and Monsieur le Count.'

There was a smattering of applause. The lights in the restaurant dimmed. The band began playing a version of 'Unforgettable' and two of the waitresses placed a small round table and a gilt chair in the middle of the dance floor which was bathed in a bright, very white light.

Nadia settled back in her chair, glancing across at Angela who was watching the dance floor intently. So far the evening was exactly what she had hoped it would be: an escape from the realities that beset her – well, one reality in particular. She had no idea what to expect next.

A woman appeared on stage. She was wearing a catsuit made from the sort of denier of nylon usually reserved for tights. It was shaded cream but hid little of her body. The woman's blonde hair was pinned tightly to her head and she was wearing heavy, dramatic make-up, especially around the eyes. In her hand she held a leather loop attached to a chain leash. As she walked on to the dance floor she tugged on the leash and a man appeared. He was dressed in black evening trousers, a white tuxedo and black bow tie, and moved on all fours like a dog, the leash attached to a studded collar strapped around his neck. The woman sat on the gilt chair, crossed her legs and tugged on the leash so the man would come to kneel in front of her.

Immediately he began kissing and licking the white high-heeled shoe on the floor while his hands caressed her ankle. Apparently satisfied with the work he had done on one, the woman put the other foot down. The man eagerly grasped it and licked the white leather. The woman opened her legs to allow him to kiss the inside of her calves and Nadia could see a lush growth of pubic hair trapped under the nylon gusset of the catsuit. Its dark colour was in contrast to the blonde hair on her head.

The man worked his hands up her legs, until they were caressing her thighs. She allowed his hands to reach up, over her hips, and then to circle her breasts. Nadia could see them clearly under the sheer nylon. They were not large and her nipples were minuscule.

She seized the leash again at the point where it was attached to the leather collar and pulled the man's face up to hers, kissing him full on the mouth.

Nadia glanced around the table. Sir George had turned his chair around to face the spectacle and was watching intently, his features wrinkled in a broad grin. Tony had not bothered to face the stage and was staring into his coffee cup. It looked as though he was blushing again. Angela sat back in her chair. She gave the impression of having seen it all before.

Nadia heard a moan of pleasure and looked back at the dance floor. The man's face was now buried between the blonde's legs and she had clamped it there firmly with her thighs, her fingers laced into his dark hair pulling him forward rhythmically as she thrust her pelvis to and fro with the same tempo. She moaned continuously, faking – or perhaps it wasn't faked – the sounds of orgasm, until she reached a crescendo and the man was pushed away, splaying back on the wooden floor.

The man got to his feet, an erection jutting from his trousers. Slowly he took off his jacket and stripped off his shirt with his back turned to the audience. In the same position he kicked off his black patent leather shoes and unzipped his trousers, letting them fall to the floor. As the trousers fell a roar of surprise came from the audience. The man was wearing black stockings and a black lace suspender belt. He turned and Nadia saw, strapped around his hips, an inflatable rubber tube that had been used to produce the erection. She also saw a pair of very female breasts. The 'man' was, in fact, a woman.

Pulling off the rubber prosthetic, the newly discovered woman lay across the table, face down, her buttocks towards the audience. The blonde got to her feet. The audience's attention had been on the 'man' but now there was yet another surprise. Sprouting from the blonde's loins, pressed up under the tight nylon, was the outline of a penis, fully erect. Freeing a hidden seam in the catsuit the blonde extracted the phallus and stroked it with her hand. How it had been hidden in the thick pubic hair Nadia did not know but there was no doubt the 'woman' was a man, or more accurately, a slim-hipped eighteen-year-old boy.

Standing behind the woman on the table the boy pushed himself between her buttocks, the erection sliding between her legs. At that moment there was a total blackout. When the lights came up again both performers had disappeared.

The audience had been so mesmerised by this turn of events they had forgotten to applaud. But that was soon remedied. Two or three of the Arabs got to their feet and began clapping wildly, the rest of the audience joining in with more circumspect appreciation.

'Jolly good, jolly good,' Sir George said, turning his chair back into the table. 'Would never have guessed. Did anyone guess? I mean, that boy made a damn fine woman. Must have been on hormones or something.'

'Definitely,' Angela agreed.

Normal service in the restaurant was resumed. A waitress arrived with a silver pot of coffee and refilled their cups. Nadia accepted Sir George's offer of a brandy and selected a Vieux Armagnac from a trolley laden with every conceivable liquor. She drank it rapidly, trying to calm herself down. The show had affected her more than she could believe. Her sex was throbbing and she knew it was moist. She felt hot and uncomfortable. Angela caught her eye and smiled knowingly, as if to confirm her reaction was the same.

'Well, shall we stay for the second act?' Sir George asked, puffing on a large Montecristo cigar.

'No, I'd like to go now,' Tony said decisively, asserting himself for the first time.

'Didn't you enjoy it, old boy?'

'No I did not. It was disgusting. Degrading. This whole place is disgusting, girls dressed like . . . like . . .'

'Just a bit of fun,' Sir George said quietly, looking a little shamefaced. 'What do you think, ladies?'

'I thought it was exciting actually,' Angela said.

'And Nadia?'

'I'd like to go,' Nadia replied, sidestepping the question.

'Righty-o. Back to my place for a nightcap then.'

No bill was presented or asked for. In a matter of minutes they had decamped to the Rolls, this time with Sir George sitting between the two women and Tony in front, his anger still simmering. Angela made it very clear to Sir George that she expected him to take full advantage of the feelings that the cabaret had aroused in her. By the time the car turned into the curved gravel driveway of a house in one of the larger avenues of Hampstead, the two were wrapped in each other's arms, the skirt of her dress rucked up around her thighs, their mouths glued together. They seemed oblivious to the fact that the car had stopped.

'We're here,' Nadia announced helpfully.

Tony had got out of the car and opened the front door, the chauffeur opening the passenger door on Nadia's side.

'Come on, old girl,' Sir George said. 'Making a bit

76

of an exhibition of ourselves . . .'

Tony took Nadia into the house, not waiting for his uncle. It was vast, a dining room capable of sitting at least thirty people on one side of the hall, a sitting room on the other. The decor was rather masculine with walnut-panelled walls and leather sofas. Pictures, lit individually by brass lamps, decorated all the walls. There was a Sickert and a Whistler in the hall and Nadia recognised another Whistler over the Adam fireplace as Tony led her into the sitting room.

'Another Armagnac?'

'Yes, please,' she said.

He went to an antique escritoire that had been converted into a drinks cabinet. He poured her brandy into a balloon glass and poured himself a Ty Nant mineral water. 'I didn't mean to be rude in the club,' he said, handing her the glass.

'You were only expressing an opinion.'

Nadia heard the front door close but neither Sir George nor Angela appeared. She thought she heard footsteps on the thick carpeting of the stairs.

'I suppose I'm just not very . . .' – he blushed again – '. . . worldly. That's why I love the classics. I'm more at home with ancient scripts.'

'I don't believe that.' Nadia heard a heavy thump from somewhere upstairs.

'It's true. I've never been very good with women.'

'Why is that?' Angela sat down on a well-used black leather Chesterfield. The split in her skirt revealed her thigh. She had had a lot to drink but whereas it usually made her woolly headed and confused, tonight it appeared to be having the reverse effect. She knew exactly what she wanted and the role she would have to perform to get it. It

77

was not a role she'd played before and that excited her.

'I don't know,' Tony was saying. 'I always seem to say the wrong things. And I never know what to do.'

'Do?'

'Like whether to hold hands or kiss her. If I kiss a girl without asking first she'll be the type who wants to be asked. If I ask first the girl's sure to be the type who wants men to be aggressive. I never get it right.'

'What type do you think I am?' Nadia said, measuring the tone of her voice precisely. She saw Tony looking at her. For the first time that evening it registered with him that Nadia was not just a companion to make up the numbers at dinner but a woman and a beautiful woman at that. Perhaps he'd imagined the age difference between them precluded anything else. As he realised it didn't he blushed a crimson red.

'I don't know,' he said, trying to hide his embarrassment by taking a long drink of water.

'Well . . .' She ran her finger around the rim of the balloon glass. She had set out this evening with the express intention of getting a man into bed. The show at the club had excited her, but the image of the woman who had pretended to be a man bent over the table naked and exposed had only added to her needs, not created them. Her desire for Tony had mounted throughout the course of the evening and now she was surprised how easy it was to translate that desire into actions. She was behaving like a man. No, that wasn't true. She doubted a man could cast the sort of spell she intended to create. 'I'm the type who likes to be very open and honest about sex. I see no point in beating about the bush.'

'No . . .' he said uncertainly.

78

'You're a very attractive man, Tony. I'm sure you don't find me unattractive.'

'You're beautiful.'

'Thank you.' She uncrossed her legs. His eyes fell to the valley of her thighs. 'So you see what I want is very simple.' She paused, letting the words hang in the air.

'What's that?'

'I'm sure this great big house has a nice comfortable bedroom with a big double bed. I'd like you to take me upstairs and . . .' She was going to say 'fuck me' but changed it to '. . . make love to me. Is that clear enough?'

'Oh yes.' He didn't look particularly delighted at the prospect. In fact he looked nervous and apprehensive. 'You *are* very beautiful.'

'I'm glad you think so.' Nadia got to her feet. She stood looking into his big serious eyes. 'I'm the type who likes to be kissed straight away,' she prompted.

'Oh . . . sorry.'

He took her cheeks in his hands and kissed her on the mouth, plunging his tongue between her lips, then wrapping his arms around her, hugging her to him, squeezing her so tight he almost took her breath away. His body was hard and strong. Nadia's sex throbbed and, for the second time that evening, she felt it moisten. Her hands caressed his buttocks; they were firm and knotted with muscle.

'Mmm . . .' she said, breaking the kiss. 'You're very strong.'

'I work out,' he said with pride.

'I love it. Come on . . .' She took his hand, enjoying the fact that she had the initiative. 'Let's find a bedroom.' She was beginning to understand how much fun Angela must have had playing the vampish role for so many years.

She led him into the hall but at the bottom of the stairs he pulled her back, circled his arms around her and kissed her again, pushing her back against one of the two elaborately carved newel posts. His tongue was hot and large. She sucked on it and felt her body pulse again. She wanted sex badly. If she had doubted that her sexual renaissance would last, she knew now the doubts were unfounded. Whatever shields had masked her receptors of pleasure, like hardened lacquer shells, had been melted away by Hamilton. The feelings just this embrace were provoking proved that. She was open and receptive now to the slightest stimulation.

Tony's penis had unfurled against her belly. It made her impatient. She broke away and took his hand again. 'Come on . . .'

They got to the top of the stairs. 'Which way?' she asked.

He led her down a corridor to the right. They passed a large pair of double doors and Nadia thought she heard Angela's voice talking softly. Tony led them through a single door at the far end of the passageway.

The large room was decorated in greens. The walls and carpet were a dark forest green while the counterpane and the upholstery of a small sofa were a check in light green and black. There were two mahogany bedside tables and two large bedside lamps with shiny green shades. Tony switched on one and used its built-in dimmer to reduce the illumination to a pleasant glow, as Nadia turned off the overhead light.

'Very comfortable,' she said, sitting on the edge of the bed. 'Is this your room?'

'God, no. I've got a little boxroom at the back for when I come to stay. I prefer that. There's a bathroom over there.' He indicated a door on the far side of the room, his nervousness very apparent.

'Why don't you undress me,' she suggested. She raised her leg and rubbed her shoe against his trousers. He stooped to pluck it off her foot. She raised the other leg and he obliged again, this time taking her foot in his hand and caressing it. 'Now my zip. It's at the back,' she said, turning to one side.

He sat on the bed behind her and found the little plastic tongue of the zip. The zip sung as it parted. His hand slipped on to her back below the strap of her bra, smoothing against her flesh.

'Why don't you undo my bra too?' she said.

His fingers fumbled with the catch, then succeeded in opening it. His hand caressed her back where the strap had been.

'You are so soft,' he said.

Nadia thought she heard Angela's voice cry out in a paroxysm of pleasure. It made her shudder. She got to her feet a little unsteadily. The feelings she was experiencing were similar to being intoxicated. She had never behaved this wantonly with any man, not even Hamilton, and it was making her giddy with excitement. She pushed her dress off her shoulders and let it fall to the floor. It made a whispering sound as the silk lining rubbed against her body and the nylon tights. She stepped out of it and picked it up, draping it over the small sofa. She shucked herself out of her bra straps and let the cups fall away, seeing his eyes looking at her breasts.

'Do you like them?' she said.

'I've never . . . they're lovely.'

Nadia walked up to the bed and stood in front of

him, so close her legs were touching his knees. Feeling her heart pumping in her chest, she ran her hand into his blond hair and pulled his face into her cleavage, holding him tightly to her bosom. He moaned.

'I'm so excited,' she said.

His hands found the waistband of her tights and began pulling them down over her hips. She released his head so he could finish the job. She was wearing black panties under the nylon, no more than a triangle of lace covering her pubic hair, supported by thin satin straps. As soon as he had wrestled the tights off her feet he straightened up, her breasts in front of his face again. This time he kissed them, one after the other, his tongue hot and wet against the spongy flesh.

'Your turn,' she said. She sat on the bed and began unbuttoning his shirt. He got to his feet, took his jacket off and wriggled out of his tie. He completed unbuttoning the shirt and pulled it off. His chest was broad with muscle lining his ribs.

'I've got to go to the loo,' he said, disappearing through the bathroom door in a flash.

Nadia got up and pulled the counterpane and bedding to the foot of the bed. The bottom sheet was cream. She propped two pillows against the mahogany headboard and rested against them. She opened her legs slightly and stroked the soft fur under the black lace of her panties. Inevitably her sex throbbed but she avoided the temptation to touch it.

When Tony emerged from the bathroom he was wearing a small white towel around his waist. His body was much beefier than it had looked in clothes, the muscles of his legs thick and well defined.

'Come over here,' Nadia said, patting the sheet beside her.

He came over to the bed and stood looking down at her. 'I'm really nervous,' he said.

'I know,' she replied quietly.

'I haven't had much experience.'

'Everyone has to start somewhere. Don't worry. Now sit down here.'

He sat down on the edge of the bed next to her. She sat up and ran her hands over his back.

'Big strong boy,' she said. She pressed her breasts into his back and he shuddered. Her nipples were as hard as pebbles. They cried out for attention. 'You're allowed to touch,' she said, lying back again.

Half turning he put his hand on the upper slope of her left breast and slowly moved it down until his finger brushed the puckered nipple.

'Mmm . . .' she said with exaggerated enthusiasm, wanting to encourage him. 'So nice . . .'

'Is it?' He rolled her nipple between his fingers more confidently. 'They're very hard.'

'I'm excited. You excite me, Tony.'

'I do?' He sounded astonished.

'Why wouldn't you? You're young, attractive, strong.'

'I try to keep really fit,' he said earnestly.

'I can see that. Why don't you take my panties off now, Tony?' she said, a huskiness creeping into her voice that reflected her excitement. She could feel her pulse rate racing and her breathing getting shallow. She scissored her legs apart until her left knee touched Tony's back. He stood up, the towel around his waist tented by his erection. Kneeling on the bed beside her he reached for the thin satin waistband on either side of her hips. As he drew it down she closed her legs and arched her buttocks off the bed. He pulled the lace clear of her sex and down her thighs. She was in such a sensitised condition even this produced a surge of feeling. Stripping the panties from her ankles he stared at the soft blonde hair that covered her mons. He ran his hand over her belly and stroked the hair as though he were stroking a little animal.

'I'm very ... I haven't ... it's just that ...' he mumbled, trying to find the right words, anxiety etched into his features.

'Sh ...' she said.

For Nadia his obvious inexperience was exciting, or was it just his youth? The aura of freshness and health he radiated, the sheen that glowed from his flesh like a perfectly ripe peach, unblemished and unwrinkled, thrilled her at a physical, animalistic level. But psychologically too there was something about his gawkiness and innocence, about the way he was looking at her, his expression torn between a sort of disbelieving adoration and raw lust.

Lust won. In one, almost balletic movement, he pulled the towel away, swung on top of her and pushed himself between her legs. She felt the crown of his erection butting into the folds of her labia. Finding the passage he plunged inside. There was no resistance. Under these circumstances Nadia did not need foreplay. Her sex was already wet.

'God,' he cried, his hand fumbling for her breast between their bodies, his face buried in her neck. 'Oh God, oh God ...'

He rode up into her, his whole body tense, his strong muscles driving his erection back and forth. He had only achieved three or four strokes when Nadia felt him shudder, a tremor so profound it affected every part of his body, and his cock spasmed inside her, jerking against the silky walls that sheathed it so tightly. He made a noise that was halfway between a sob of despair and a cry of anger and immediately rolled off her. He lay on his side with his back towards her, curling his legs into a foetal position.

His attack had been so sudden, and ended so quickly, Nadia had barely had time to react. His cock had felt wonderful for the few seconds it was inside her, hard and strong and big, but she needed more, much more. She considered getting up and going home. But what would that achieve? Her frustration, the needs that had sent her out hunting in the first place, would only be compounded.

'I'm sorry,' he muttered.

'For what?' she said gently. It was certainly no good being angry with him. He needed coaxing. Young boys were supposed to have phenomenal recovery rates, weren't they? Wasn't that one of the advantages of younger men, according to the various magazines aimed at the liberated woman? Well, it was time to put the theory to the test.

'I mean . . . I just couldn't . . .'

'Sh . . . you felt wonderful, Tony.' She turned on her side and pressed her body into his, spooning it against him. She didn't know whether she was acting cynically in her own interests or genuinely trying to spare the boy's feelings. It didn't matter. The result would, hopefully, be the same. 'You just got over-excited. It's a terrific compliment.'

'I just . . .'

'Sh . . .' she insisted. 'There's no hurry. Now it's my turn.'

'What do you mean?'

'Does this feel good?' She pressed her firm breasts into his naked back.

'Yes,' he said without conviction.

'Can you feel my nipples?' She squirmed her breasts against his shoulder blades.

'Mmm . . .' he said with rather more interest.

Nadia ran her hand around to his chest and found his nipple. She flicked it with her fingernail, then pinched it between the nails of her thumb and forefinger quite hard. She felt him react, his body trembling.

'Nice?' she asked, moving over to the other nipple and giving it the same treatment.

'Yes,' he acknowledged with surprise.

She kissed his neck and let him feel her hot wet tongue against his skin. Nadia had never played the seductress before and had never thought of herself as particularly experienced sexually. But compared with his total inexperience she knew enough to give him the impression he was in the hands of an expert. She brought her mouth up to his ear, bit his lobe then pushed her tongue deep into the inner whorls.

Emerging from his foetal cocoon, he straightened his legs. Nadia pushed her belly against his buttocks and felt them push back in return. She rubbed her thighs together, squeezing her clitoris between her labia. It felt as hard as her nipples. Her labia were wet and she could feel a trail of moisture leaking on to her thigh.

Gently she rolled Tony on to his back and came up on to her knees at his side. She saw his eyes looking at her breasts and held them both in her hands, pinching her own nipples as she had done his. His cock stirred very slightly.

'Open your legs,' she said.

'What for?' He sounded momentarily like a petulant schoolboy. She cast the image aside quickly, not wanting it to interfere with her scenario.

'Just do as I say.'

He spread his legs apart. Nadia shifted down the bed and knelt between them. It must have been obvious what she planned to do because he said immediately, 'I don't think I can . . .'

'Sh . . .'

'But really . . .'

'You have no choice,' she said sternly, surprised at her own decisiveness. 'I told you, it's my turn.'

His guilt made him unable to argue with that assertion and he lay still, his eyes torn between pleading with her to stop and studying her breasts.

Nadia leant forward, took his cock in her hand and fed it into her mouth. She tasted her own juices. She sucked it all in. Not satisfied with that, she captured his balls between her lips too.

Tony moaned. His hands went to her head as if to pull her away but then he felt a sudden quiver of excitement from his cock as Nadia's tongue licked the pronounced ridge at the base of his glans. The quiver became a spasm, the spasm a steady pulse. Slowly and inexorably, as Nadia worked her hot wet tongue over the same spot, his cock began to engorge.

'Mmm . . .' she muttered, wanting him to know she could feel it.

'Yes . . .' he said in wonder at his own achievement.

It was only a matter of seconds before his erection filled her mouth and she could no longer contain his balls. They spilled from her lips one by one, as she

87

concentrated on the rest of his phallus. He was hard now, and throbbing. For a moment he pulsed so strongly she thought he was going to come again. But he didn't. The convulsions came under control.

'So good,' he said.

She pulled her mouth away, holding his shaft firmly in her hand, proud of her creation. 'You see,' she said. He had passed the test. It was true what they said about young men.

'You're wonderful,' he told her. His attitude changed with his erection, his confidence in his masculinity miraculously restored.

'It's still my turn,' Nadia reminded him.

'Yes.'

She moved forward, straddling his hips until her sex was poised above his cock. She guided it between her labia and used it to stroke her clitoris. She felt a jolt of pure pleasure so powerful it forced her eyes closed and almost made her lose balance. She stuck out her hand to steady herself against his belly.

'You're a very sexy man,' she said, whether for his benefit or hers she was not sure. She squeezed his cock in her hand to test its hardness. It was adamantine.

Tony bucked his hips, anxious to get inside her, but Nadia resisted. She wanted to tease herself first, feel the sensation flowing out of her clitoris as she stroked it against the smoothness and heat of his glans. She had been so concerned to resurrect Tony's erection she had not thought of herself. It was nice now to be able to revel in her body's sensitivity. It felt so alive and so sexy. That was the difference from what she had felt in the past. Not only did she want sex – she had always *wanted* it –

but now she seemed to have the ability to satisfy her own desires. Her body was all charged up, sensitised and sensitive to every provocation.

'Do you want me?' she said.

'You know I do.' He reached up and took her breasts in his hands, trying to use them to pull her down on him.

At that moment she heard a loud scream of ecstasy, hardly muffled by the intervening walls. It was the word 'yes' repeated three times in quick succession, the sound so distorted by passion it was hardly a word at all.

That was the last straw for Nadia: she could hold out no longer. For a second, in her mind's eye she saw Angela being taken by Sir George. She saw it quite graphically, her friend lying on her back with her legs sticking up in the air in a giant V, Sir George buried at the apex of the angle. She could see the expression on Angela's face, her eyes wild, her mouth open and slack with passion. Instantly she dropped herself on to Tony's hard phallus. It rammed into her, filling the depths of her vagina, taking her breath away, and provoking a surge of feeling that shook her to the core.

She squirmed down on the sword of flesh inside her, taking possession of it, making it her own. All the old feelings were revived. Not that they were really old at all. She had wondered if any man could make her feel what Hamilton had made her feel. Now she knew even this callow boy could. Hamilton had been the progenitor of her passion but was not its sole master.

Instantly Nadia felt the first stirrings of orgasm, not muted, distant feelings, a ghost that had to be searched out, but wild, rich currents of sensation, pounding in her blood so strongly that the gap between the realisation that her body had begun the circle of climax and the climax itself was only a matter of seconds.

Driving herself down on Tony's hard cock, spreading her legs apart so her clitoris could grind against his pubic bone, using every muscle to push him into her, Nadia's orgasm flooded over the crown of his cock. Her sex seemed to open, as though there were a secret barrier, another level into which he was permitted only as she came. It was more real than imagined perhaps but it added impetus to the core of feeling that raced through her.

Before she knew what was happening, before she'd even begun to regain her senses, Tony seized her by the shoulders, rolled her over on to her side and then on to her back and fell on top of her, plunging his temporarily disconnected cock back into her sex. He began pumping to and fro, arching his whole body to push deeper then pulling back until his glans was kissed by her nether lips. Not satisfied with this, he grabbed her legs under her knees and pushed her thighs back towards her torso, changing the angle of her sex and enabling him to penetrate deeper still.

Suddenly he stopped dead. Nadia felt his cock pulsing inside her. She thought he was going to come. He thought he was too. He lay perfectly still, trying to control himself, before gingerly beginning to move again. The pulsing eased. He moved slightly faster, testing himself. His confidence grew. He was in control again and every stroke proved it. He pumped as hard as he had before with no loosening of the bonds of restraint. It was a major victory. It made him feel powerful and masculine. Using his well-trained muscles he plunged deep, as deep as before, but though the clinging, hot, velvety walls of her sex gave him exquisite pleasure as he stroked against them, though the temptation to press his glans into the absolute depths of her and spill his seed was almost irresistible, it could be resisted. He was a man now, not a boy.

'Yes,' he said triumphantly.

'Tony, Tony,' Nadia muttered.

Almost before her first orgasm had faded a second broke over her. She wrapped her arms around his back and clung to him as though she were drowning, her body quivering with feeling. His muscles were like steel. It was not only his cock that was hard. His whole body was like a giant phallus.

'I could feel that,' he said proudly, his belief in his own prowess flooding through him as strongly as his pleasure.

Nadia wallowed in her feelings, squirming and writhing under Tony's body, tossing her head from side to side, loving it all. Suddenly she found herself seeing Hamilton, looking into his mahogany eyes. They were looking at her knowingly as if to say, 'I told you so'. She remembered that first night, how he'd used the tip of his finger to circle and tease her clitoris. She remembered the absolute shock of the pleasure that she'd felt.

She tried to put the image aside, tried to concentrate on Tony and forget about Hamilton. But there was no escape. His eyes hypnotised her. Like the spectre at the feast he lingered. She heard his voice questioning her. 'Isn't it me you really want?' it said.

'Yes, yes,' she cried aloud, hoping the words would rid her of the ghost.

But they didn't. He was inside her. As Tony's cock pressed ever deeper into her sex, opening her out, it was Jack Hamilton who really possessed her, whose throbbing erection was making her come again, whose hands held her legs so firmly, whose mouth sucked at the long sinews of her neck, who pitched her into orgasm and made her scream for release.

He was coming inside her. She felt his cock begin to throb again but this time he did not try to stop it. His pace slowed then stopped completely. Involuntarily Nadia's body convulsed around him, clinging to his hardness like a limpet. A spasm jerked his cock violently inside her, then another. Semen jetted out of him.

Nadia was defenceless against it. He had opened her up completely, exposed the raw nerves. Each jet hit her with the force of a tidal wave, throwing her back, pitching her into an abyss of pleasure. She screamed again, this time with sheer delight.

'Jack, Jack, Jack,' echoed in her mind, though whether she screamed the words out loud she could not tell.

Chapter Five

'THAT'S HIM.'

Kurt Froebel was indicating a man sitting on his own at a large window table. They were in Le Grand Chiffre just off Bishopsgate, a purpose-built restaurant on the top floor of one of the most lavish new office developments in the city. Its plate-glass windows overlooked a throng of city workers busily going about their short lunch breaks, rushing around the streets with little packets of sandwiches.

Andrew Anderson was a small, slender man with a beautifully tailored grey suit, a blue handmade shirt and a patterned Sulka silk tie. His black shoes were handmade too. He had neatly cut short fair hair that was greying over the ears and a rather feminine face with a small nose and chin and soft, dove grey eyes.

'Introduce me then,' Nadia prompted. She had dressed for the occasion, a St Laurent flannel suit in a Prince of Wales check.

Kurt Froebel attracted the attention of one of the waiters, who was dressed *à la française*: white shirt, black trousers and a white linen *tablier* tied around his waist.

'Take Mr Anderson a glass of champagne with my compliments, would you?'

'Certainly, sir.'

They were standing by the bar at the far side of the restaurant. The waiter ordered the champagne from the barman, placed the glass on his silver tray and marched over to Anderson's table. They saw him gesturing towards Froebel, obviously indicating whence the drink had come. Anderson immediately gestured for Kurt to come over.

'Kurt, how are you?' he said as soon as they were in earshot. He got up from the table and shook Froebel's hand.

'Andrew, nice to see you, old friend. May I introduce Ms Irving?'

'How formal,' Nadia mocked. 'Nadia Irving,' she corrected, holding out her hand. Anderson shook it lightly, his grip rather weak.

'Won't you join me? Kurt and I go back a long way, Ms Irving.' He emphasised the 'ms'.

'Nadia, please.'

'What a lovely name.'

'My parents were great romantics.'

'Please, you must sit down.'

'Actually, I have to rush,' Kurt said. The introduction made, they had agreed he would make himself scarce.

'Let's have lunch soon. Give me a ring,' Anderson said.

'Love to.' Kurt bowed slightly then winged his way across the restaurant.

'I must go too,' Nadia said.

'Please stay. I always seem to end up eating lunch

on my own. It would be nice to have company.'

'It's very kind of you but I really ought to go.'

'And if I insist?'

He summoned a passing waiter who pulled a chair out from the table, waiting for Nadia to sit down. With what she thought was an appropriate show of reluctance she gracefully acquiesced.

'A drink?' Anderson asked while the waiter still hovered.

'I don't drink at lunchtime.' She noticed the bottle of mineral water on the table.

'Neither do I, but as Kurt has bought me a glass of champagne I certainly don't intend to waste it. Join me in one glass and then we'll be good.'

'You've convinced me.'

Anderson nodded to the hovering waiter. Nodding his understanding, the waiter hurried away.

'So what can I do for you, Ms Irving?' he said, pointedly changing the mood.

'What do you mean?'

'Oh please, you wouldn't have gone to all the trouble of dragging Kurt in here to get yourself introduced if you didn't want something from me. Poor man's not even allowed to have any lunch.' He had seen through the subterfuge immediately but was intrigued. He also found Nadia an extremely attractive woman.

'Very astute.'

'That's what I get paid for. So?'

'I work for Hill Brothers . . .'

'Oh, I see.' His face clouded with anger. 'Well, in that case I think we'd better make small talk and have a very quick lunch.'

'Can I just ask you one question?'

'No, Ms Irving, you can't.'

'Did you know,' she continued regardless, 'that Manny Tomkins is going to drop his entire holding into our lap?'

'Manny told me personally he was absolutely committed to me.'

'Manny is a two-timing shit. The whole city knows that.'

'True,' he conceded.

'It is agreed. That gives Manson's control.'

'So if you've already got control, why come to me?'

'Because I see another alternative.'

'What's that?'

'That our clients don't take you over at all.'

The anger on Anderson's face dissipated as the waiter arrived with Nadia's champagne.

'Tell me more,' he said as soon as the waiter had gone.

'Our clients want an aggregates company, *any* aggregates company. It's a good fit for their business, lots of synergy, economies of scale, and distribution.'

'I've heard the pitch.'

'But you're not the right company. You're too big. If they mount a hostile takeover their gearing will go sky high. They have three institutional shareholders who I know would start getting very unhappy about their holdings.'

'Why tell me this?'

'Because I want to do the best for my clients. If they end up with your company but with a falling share price compounded by all the publicity of a hostile bid, they are not going to be very happy.'

'I should give a damn.'

'But you should. You own a holding in Babcock Minerals, don't you?'

'You've done your homework.'

'Babcock's is exactly the right fit for Manson's – not too big, and the right mines in the right places.'

'Go on.'

'Babcock's is controlled by a family trust. They hold sixty-six per cent. It's takeover-proof. That's why its share price hasn't moved in ten years.'

'I wish I was in the same position.'

'No you don't. Your share price has quadrupled in the last five years. Your share options alone made you one-point-six million last year.'

'You *have* done your homework.'

'So all you have to do is persuade Babcock's to sell to Manson's.'

'Look, Ms Irving, this is all very commendable work, but do you really think that if I could get Charlie Babcock to sell I wouldn't have done it already? It's a non-starter. He wouldn't sell at any price.'

'Charlie Babcock is an old man. His son is ambitious. Very ambitious.'

'But,' he said, as though trying to explain to a ten-year-old child, 'it's a trust. His son can't sell without the whole family's consent.'

Nadia paused for dramatic effect. 'He can,' she said after a long beat. 'Put it another way. Nora Babcock is dead.'

'What!' Anderson's voice was so loud it startled the diners at the next table. 'How do you know that?' he snapped.

'She was in a sanatorium in Switzerland. They buried her there.'

'Unbelievable. You sure about this?'

'I've a friend in Geneva. She's married to a doctor, Nora Babcock's doctor.'

'It changes everything. Charlie's lost control.

Jesus, I've been trying to get hold of that company for years.'

'So give it to Manson's and they're off your back. They only need to offer the son a good job, share options, all the usual perks. He'll take it like a shot.'

Anderson looked at her intently. 'Why didn't you just take this straight to Manson's?'

'Firstly they might not have taken kindly to being told they were biting off more than they could chew.'

'And secondly?'

'You own a good chunk of the shares. I'd like to do a deal for them. And thirdly . . .'

'Yes?'

'I thought you'd be grateful.'

'How grateful?'

'Grateful enough to transfer all your business to Hill Brothers.'

'Done,' he said immediately, picking up the glass of champagne and beaming like a man who had just had a death sentence lifted. She raised her glass too and clinked it against his. 'On one condition.'

'What's that?' she asked.

'That you have dinner with me next week.'

'No conditions,' she said firmly.

'All right, no conditions. So will you have dinner with me next week?'

'I'll think about it. Can we order? I appear to have developed a very healthy appetite.'

James Hill burst into her office without knocking. He was middle-aged, running to fat and had pernicious bad breath. He obviously didn't have a friend in the world to tell him about it.

'Where have you been?' he said.

'At lunch,' she said.

'It's four o'clock.'

'I was just coming to see you,' Nadia said calmly, ignoring his anger. 'I think it's time we discussed my contract.'

'If you're going to stay out at lunch till four . . .'

'Three-thirty,' she corrected. 'I was back at three-thirty.'

'Three-thirty then. If that's what you think we pay you for then I think it's definitely time we discussed your contract.'

'I was having lunch with Andrew Anderson.'

'What?'

'You heard.'

'Anderson. What was the point of that?'

'And then I rang George Manson. You're expected there at five.'

'What are you talking about?'

'Anderson is going to sell his Babcock shares to Manson. Manson's is going to buy Babcock's instead of Anderson's.'

'What?'

'You heard.'

'But it's not possible.'

'It's a done deal.'

'It's absolutely brilliant, that's what it is,' he said as the implications of what she had told him sank in.

Helpfully, she spelled them out for him. 'The institutions won't worry any more. Manson's share price will rocket and so will Anderson's. And Anderson's going to bring all his business to us.'

James Hill looked nonplussed. 'Come to my office in fifteen minutes,' he said brusquely. 'I need to talk to my brother.'

'Certainly, sir,' she said emphasising the 'sir' with a degree of irony.

If Angela had answered her phone it wouldn't have happened. Not that night anyway. Perhaps it was inevitable, like the invisible attraction of a magnet, something she could not resist. She would have been pulled back inexorably in the end. But more immediately, as Angela wasn't in, Nadia had no one to celebrate with.

She sat at her kitchen table feeling sorry for herself, when that was the last thing she should have been feeling. James and Cameron Hill had agreed she would join the board of Hill Brothers in November. From that time she would have a share option package and a percentage of the profits. Her plan had worked out perfectly. Manson's were delighted and, so, after she had talked again on the phone to him, was Andrew Anderson. The Hills had had no choice but to concede graciously that it was a considerable coup and to reward her endeavour accordingly. Nadia Irving was the toast of the city. But she had no one to propose the toast.

She could have called Tony, of course. But though physically their encounter had, eventually, been a success she had no intention of getting involved with someone so much younger than herself. She had told him there could be no future for them and he had accepted it reluctantly but without argument. If she called him now and started the whole thing up again it might not be so easy to disentangle herself. She had used Tony for her own purposes. He was a distraction, nothing more.

She picked up the phone and dialled the number, then crashed the receiver down before it started to ring. Her secretary had noted each of his three calls on pages torn from a little yellow message pad which she had left on her desk, as any call to her at Hill Brothers would have been. Without consciously wanting to, she had remembered the call back number, presumably the number of his studio, not his home. She dialled it again. She was just about to crash the receiver down for a second time and curse herself for her foolishness when she heard the line begin to ring.

'Hello,' he answered on the second ring. She had forgotten the sound of his voice. It was rich and melodic like the low register of a viola.

'It's Nadia,' she said weakly, not having prepared what she was going to say.

'Oh . . .' He didn't sound pleased to hear from her.

'I'm sorry I didn't . . . I've been . . .'

'What do you want?' he snapped.

'To see you.' She couldn't think of any other way to put it.

'Why didn't you call me back?'

'I had to sort myself out, Jack.'

'What does that mean?'

There was no way she could avoid the truth. 'I didn't know you were married. I wasn't sure what my attitude was. I had to work it out.' There was a silence at the other end of the line. 'Now I have,' she said, rushing to fill the vacuum.

'I understand.' His voice softened.

'Would you like to have dinner?'

'Yes. Why not? When had you got in mind?'

'Actually I just had some good news at work. I was thinking of celebrating.'

'Tonight?'

'Yes.'

'All right. Shall I come to you or do you want to come here?'

Nadia suddenly saw the ruffled bed in the studio. She shuddered and felt her sex pulse.

'Why don't you come here? There's a good restaurant . . .'

'Not a restaurant,' he said definitely, with no explanation.

'I could cook something then.'

'That would be good. I'll bring the champagne.'

'Done.' She remembered Andrew Anderson saying the same word over lunch. It was a word that had already changed her life. She jerked herself back to the present and told Jack her address.

'What time?'

'Eight.' It was just gone six.

'Fine.' She heard him hesitate. 'And Nadia . . .'

'Yes.'

'I'm glad you rang.'

'So am I,' she said but as she put the phone down realised she was not at all sure that it was true.

But she was committed now. There was no going back. She looked in the fridge and decided she needed to get some food. There was a supermarket around the corner and she ran out of the house, glad of the distraction of dreaming up a meal, saving her from thinking about the consequences of what she had done. She needed something simple and easy to prepare.

In an hour and a half she had done the shopping, set the table in the dining room at the back of the kitchen and prepared the food. She had twenty minutes to prepare herself. She had a quick shower and put on her make-up, while she thought what to wear. It needed to be simple, like the food, and easy to discard. She opened her lingerie drawers. What she was going to wear underneath had to be considered too. After all, she thought, hardening herself to the idea, she was about to embark on an affair with a married man. Sex was its *raison d'être*. It was too late to agonise over whether she should or she shouldn't. That was a decision she had already made.

Her doorbell rang at five minutes past eight. She looked out of her bedroom window and saw a black cab pulling away from the curb. She checked her hair in the mirror. She had chosen a waisted red dress with a flared skirt. It was very plain but the colour suited her blonde hair and the style her narrow waist and the fullness of her bosom and hips. She walked downstairs, trying to keep calm and avoid the temptation to run. She could not stop her heart pounding against her ribs.

'Hi,' she said opening the door.

'Hi.' Hamilton stood on the front step. He was wearing very clean faded blue jeans, docksider shoes in light blue and a military-style beige shirt, with breast pockets on both sides. He held a plastic carrier bag in one hand.

'Come in.'

Rather self-consciously she kissed him on the cheek.

'This is nice,' he said looking around, examining the lithographs she had on the wall.

'Come through.' She led him through the kitchen and dining room and out into her small patio garden where she had laid a small cast-iron table with a flowery green cloth. She'd put out two champagne glasses, a wine cooler filled with ice and a bowl of black olives.

'Shall I open the champagne?' he said, extracting a bottle of Moët Chandon champagne from the off-licence carrier bag. He opened it expertly with no fuss, twisting the cork out without a pop and pouring the wine into the glasses. She picked them both up and handed him one as he slid the bottle into the ice of the cooler.

'Cheers,' she said.

'Cheers,' he repeated, meeting her gaze briefly. 'So tell me what we're celebrating.' He sat down on the little white cast-iron bench that matched the two chairs positioned around the table.

'Just a coup at work. It's not very interesting.'

'Tell me,' he insisted.

She did. To her surprise he seemed genuinely fascinated, asking her questions about how family trusts worked and why the institutions had been so against Manson's taking over Anderson's. She found herself explaining the technical details of gearing and prices to income ratios.

'No wonder they've given you a directorship,' he commented when she'd finished.

'It was just luck really, finding out about Nora Babcock.'

'Don't put yourself down,' he said.

He got up and wandered around the garden, looking at all the plants, naming most of them and even telling her where they originated in the world.

'You know a lot about plants,' she said.

'Good for the soul,' he replied.

She had the feeling there was a vast chasm between them, a lack of spontaneity, that had not been there on the night they had met. She knew it was a chasm she had created but suddenly felt resentful that *she* was being put in the position of having to bridge it. She had thought she could hold her anger at him in check and rely on her passion, but he appeared to feel it was she who should say sorry.

'Do you have a soul?' she snapped.

He looked at her long and hard, then sat down on the cast-iron bench. 'Sit here with me,' he said softly.

'I'm not sure I want to,' she said like a petulant child, her mood entirely changed.

'Please, Nadia. There's something I want to explain.'

Nadia sipped her champagne, then sat down next to him. He turned towards her, those big brown eyes dazzling her again.

'So what upset you?'

'You're married. Why didn't you tell me?'

'I assumed you knew. It was in the art gallery profile.'

'I know.'

'Nadia, I didn't lie to you.'

'How many affairs have you had?'

'That's a silly question. I hope I'm selective.'

'Oh, I'm sure you are.' Nadia practically spat the words out.

'Look, perhaps this is a bad idea.'

'Yes, I think it is.' She hadn't thought beyond her lust. She wanted him more than she'd ever wanted any man. Not an hour had gone by without her thinking about him and craving for him. She'd thought she could cope with the fact that he was married to someone else, that she was and would only ever be a casual affair, that, above all, he was the sort of man who could betray his wife, but she couldn't. She couldn't respect him. She had felt all these emotions before with Jeffrey Allen, trying to kid herself that she didn't care, trying not to face the unpalatable facts for the sake of being with him.

He put his glass down, got up and walked through the French windows into the house.

'Don't go,' she said. She had felt all these emotions before with Jeffrey but he had inspired no sexual passion. She caught up with him in the kitchen.

'I thought . . .'

'For Christ's sake, Jack, just fuck me. Fuck me, Jack, please.' She threw herself into his arms, a flood of emotion washing over her. As she kissed him full on the lips, as their tongues met, both wanting to penetrate the other's mouth, as his arms wrapped around her and crushed her into his body, Nadia experienced the whole gamut of emotions: hatred, self-loathing, fear, anger and resentment, but most of all passion, a passion that coursed through her body like a crimson tide, a tsunami of passion that swept everything else away.

'Jack, Jack . . .' she said while their mouths were still joined, her tongue and lips moving against him.

He hoisted her into his arms, as if her weight was of no account, cradling her like a baby. He started upstairs.

'It's two floors,' she protested, breaking the kiss, but he had already breasted the first flight. He took the second at the same speed.

In her bedroom he laid her on the bed, not at all out of breath. Then he was kissing her again, rolling on top of her, pushing his hard body down against her softness, crushing her breasts. His hand worked up her leg, caressing her thigh.

'Are you going to fuck me, Jack?' she asked

unnecessarily, but wanting to hear the words.

'Yes.'

He rolled on his side and began unbuttoning the front of her dress. She wrestled with his belt. The fly of his jeans was buttoned and she yanked it open easily. She reached inside and grabbed his cock, pulling it from the front of his crisp white boxer shorts. There was no time to be civilised, to get up and undress and fold their clothes away.

He freed the buttons of her dress and laid it open. Nadia was wearing a black satin teddy, with lace cups over her breasts. His hands kneaded the pliant flesh as Nadia found the clasps that held the crotch in place. She felt the heat and ripeness of her sex as she tore the fastenings apart. He rolled on top of her again, his cock nudging into her labia.

'Let me . . .' she gasped, pulling at his jeans and shorts. He raised himself from her body so she could wrestle them down over his buttocks but as soon as they were clear of his cock he fell back on to her. In one fluid stroke he was deep inside her sex.

'God,' she cried in surprise. It was surprise at herself. She had never been so wet. She felt as though her vagina was flooded.

'You see,' he whispered, knowing the effect he had on her.

'You bastard,' she said, hating him again. She tried to squirm away from him, but the movement only increased the rush of feeling his cock was creating. 'You bastard,' she said again, this time because the words excited her. Whatever he had done to her body, whatever key he had found in the depths of her libido, the door he had unlocked with it was wide open. Already the inescapable momentum of orgasm had started forward.

He didn't do much. He seemed able to sense what she needed. He just pressed forward, the muscles of his buttocks holding his cock deep inside her, up against the neck of her womb.

He was so hard. So hot and hard. He seemed to fill her completely as though he had been carefully moulded to fit every crevice of her sex. Her orgasm gathered impetus. He was supporting himself on his elbows, looking down into her face. She looked into his eyes.

'Kiss me,' she said, her resentment melted away by the heat of him inside her.

He dipped his head immediately, kissing her very gently on the lips. At the exact moment the wave of her orgasm broke over her, his tongue plunged between her lips, in imitation of his cock. She gasped, her hot breath expelled into his mouth, as she clung to him for support, her body trembling uncontrollably. Teasingly he withdrew his tongue and kissed her with his lips, with the lightest of touches, the sweet delicacy of it in such contrast to the pounding waves of pleasure from her sex. As she felt her body relax, the tension of her climax draining away, he broke the kiss.

'I wanted you too,' he said softly, beginning to pump his cock in and out of her. He dropped his mouth to her neck and began kissing and licking at her flesh. 'I wanted you very much.' He was moving gently but firmly, the hard phallus surrounded by the clinging glove of her vagina.

Nadia raised her legs, bending her knees, angling her pelvis up at him, wanting to give him pleasure now. She ran her hands down the back of his shirt and on to his naked buttocks, caressing them, then turning her fingers into talons to urge him on. But she was not immune. The feeling of his hardness sliding in and out of her was too provoking. In her fevered imagination it seemed she could feel every inch of him, every contour of his erection, every ridge and vein. She could certainly feel his balls slapping against her labia. They were heavy and full.

'You're making me come again,' she told him.

'I know, I can feel it,' he said.

'Do you want it?'

'Yes.' He crushed his body down against her in response, writhing his chest against her breasts, making her nipples prick with feeling. Her orgasm took hold of her, like the hand of a giant picking up a rag doll, and shook her violently, overwhelming her with raw sensation. But, at the centre of it all, at the moment she thought it could not be any more exquisite, she felt him find a place in her sex. Almost of its own accord her vagina seemed to open around him and close on him too, at the same time, trapping him as his cock began to spasm and semen spattered out into the cache it had created.

They were both gasping for breath. Sweating, their clothes making them hot. Coming up for air, they disentangled themselves, lying, exhausted, side by side, with not enough energy to discard the clothes that were uncomfortably rucked around their bodies.

Nadia only realised she must have dozed off when she woke up having trouble, for a second, remembering where she was. She saw Hamilton was asleep too, his face turned towards her. He looked like a little boy, the wrinkles and tensions of age dissolved by the effects of sleep, not a care invading his world.

Getting off the bed without disturbing him, she tiptoed into the bathroom and stripped off the damp and crumpled dress, then pulled the satin teddy over her head. The bathroom was cooler than the bedroom, where the sun streamed in through the west-facing windows at the end of the day. Naked she sat on the loo, the effects of passion giving way to a thinking woman's doubts. Sex had never ruled her life before; she had never allowed it to compromise her, or make her do things she found reprehensible. On the other hand she had never had sex like this before.

'What are you doing?' his voice said from the bedroom.

'Trying to cool down.'

He appeared in the bathroom doorway. 'Let's take a shower.'

'Good idea.'

She got up, opened the shower cubicle and adjusted the mixer tap until the water ran lukewarm, all the time aware of his eyes on her body. She stepped into the stream of water as he stripped off his clothes. The water cascaded over her, splashing on the ridge of her breasts, running down her body to be funnelled by the creases of her pelvis into her pubic hair.

He stepped in behind her and closed the cubicle door. Immediately she felt his hands cupping her wet breasts and his navel pressing against the sharp curves of her buttocks.

'You feel so good, so soft,' he whispered in her ear. 'I needed you so badly.'

Like you need your wife, she thought but did not say. How could she let herself do this? The answer unfurled between her buttocks. It appeared it was

110

not only the young who could recover with alacrity. The feeling of his erection growing against her, such tangible proof of his desire, made her sex pulse.

He picked up a bar of soap from the little metal tray at the side of the tap and began running it over the front of her body, up around her neck, all over her breasts, down to her belly and over her thighs, the lather it created making her body slippery and soft. He moved it to her mons then down between her thighs, the edge of the soap parting her labia, catching against her clitoris.

'Oh . . .' she moaned.

He pulled back from her and brought the soap around to lather her shoulders and her spine and the pliant flesh of her buttocks, running it down the back of her thighs then up between her legs again. The lather was thick and white.

'You're so beautiful,' he said, pushing into her back again.

'Please . . .' she said, water splashing on her face. She didn't know whether it meant please stop or please take me again. Her body was less ambiguous. It was rocking against him, her buttocks moving rhythmically.

His cock slipped down between her legs. The water had washed away all her natural juices and, perversely, made her dry. He tried to force himself up into her sex but she was sealed against him.

'Have to force it,' he said.

'Yes, do that.'

She felt the tip of his glans prodding at the gate of her vagina. It managed to force past the initial resistance. Beyond, on the inside, was a lake of sticky wetness, as hot as molten lava. It lubricated his cock instantly and allowed him to push deeply into the centre of her.

'Lovely,' he said.

He used the tapered edge of the soap to open her labia, then rubbed it against her clitoris. Water running down her body caught on the soap and was directed on to the nut of her clit, forming a lather as he moved it. The feeling of it slipping and sliding against her was delicious.

He was making her come again, so quickly, with so little effort. Standing like this the penetration of his phallus in her sex was not deep but all she needed was the feeling of the breadth of him, stretching her labia apart. She braced herself against the cubicle with her arms, needing support, as her body churned.

'Oh God . . .'

'Feels good,' he said.

'Oh Jack, what have you done to me?'

She wriggled her buttocks from side to side. He cupped her breast with his free hand and pinched her nipple. The soap worked relentlessly. It was so easy. Like the first time with him. In seconds she felt herself buzzing, her clitoris spewing out feeling into the rest of her nerves, her orgasm rising like a flood tide, forcing her eyes closed, its eddies and currents carrying her helplessly into a whirlpool of pleasure, the water hammering down on her body only increasing the illusion that she could drown in exquisite sensation.

As her senses returned he opened the cubicle door and pulled her out. Even if she had wanted to resist she had no energy. She had no energy even to stand and he carried her, dripping wet, into the bedroom. He lowered her on to the bed then rolled her over on to her stomach, pulling her up on to her knees and kneeling behind. His hard cock prodded into the cleft of her buttocks again. Instantly he slipped inside her, deeper inside this time, deeper than he'd been all evening.

She felt his cock pulse. He stroked it in and out slowly, feeling the way her wet flesh parted to admit him, folding around him, then closing on itself again as he withdrew.

'So lovely,' he said, 'like silk.'

'Oh, Jack.' It was like when he kissed her earlier, so infinitely gentle, so sweet. Her wild swings of emotion were out of control. She'd gone from hatred to anger to lust and now to what felt like tenderness. She would have done anything for him.

'Let me do it,' she said decisively.

'Do what?' he said.

'Do anything, Jack, anything you want.'

'I want this. You feel wonderful.'

He didn't stop. His pulsing erection stroked forward. She reached down between his legs and caught the sac of his balls in her hand. She squeezed it gently and his cock reacted, jerking strongly in her sex.

'Like this?' she asked, delighted to have found a way to please him.

'Oh yes . . .'

'Come then.' She knew at once she had the power to make him come for her. She squeezed harder and pulled the sac down away from his body.

'Oh yes.'

She felt his cock spasm. She squeezed once more and, as though she were milking the spunk out of him, his cock erupted, jerking wildly inside her for the second time, his spending seemingly as urgent and as copious as the first.

They sat in the garden drinking the champagne. They had picked at the food Nadia had prepared but ended up eating no more than salad and cheese. It was a balmy night and Nadia felt perfectly comfortable in the short white cotton robe she'd wrapped herself in to cook the meal. Oddly she seemed to have come to terms with the problem she had wrestled with all night. It didn't seem to matter any more. Her body was sexually replete, the aftermath of the shocks of sensation that Hamilton had provoked leaving her with a sense of contentment that nothing could disturb. Or so she thought.

'Tell me about your wife?' she said, as if to test herself, to see whether her new-found indifference would last.

'She's very beautiful,' Hamilton said. He had put on his jeans and shirt but left the latter unbuttoned.

'Yes.' Nadia had seen the latest set of pictures, a fashion layout in *Vogue* – dresses and suits in black and white, the colours of the new autumn season. Jan Hamilton had long legs and a small but shapely bosom. Her face was angular and sharp and inimitably photogenic. 'And?' she asked.

'She's not like you. She's quite cold, actually. And unforgiving.'

'She knows you have affairs? I'd like the truth.'

'Oh yes. She has them too. Sometimes we share,' he said, almost as an aside.

Nadia thought he was joking. 'Very convenient.'

'My wife is bisexual.'

It took a minute for Nadia to connect the remark with the idea of sharing. When she did her reply exploded, 'You share lovers!'

'Yes. You said you wanted the truth.'

She had failed the test. She found that her hand was trembling and her heart beating at an accelerated pace. She gulped at her champagne.

'In the same bed?' She tried but did not succeed in keeping her voice at a normal pitch.

'Sometimes.' He looked unfazed.

Nadia felt she had stepped into quicksand and was sinking rapidly.

He could read the expression on her face. 'There are no rules, Nadia. Life can be very complicated, *is* very complicated. Women are liberated now. Look at you. Even ten years ago a woman wouldn't have done your job; it just wouldn't have been allowed.'

'What's that got to do with it?'

'Everything. Women have taken responsibility for themselves. They're allowed to express their own desires, not have them subordinated to the desires of men. That's what you did with me, after all. It seems churlish for men to object after so long in the driving seat.'

Nadia suspected that was just intellectual sophistry, but she was too emotionally involved to argue logically. 'How many lovers do you have?'

'Jointly? Not many.'

'And singularly?'

'It's not a competition.'

'Are you happy?'

He laughed. 'Happy. That's a bit bourgeois, isn't it?'

'Will you stay together?' Nadia persisted.

He had been looking at a big rhododendron bush that grew in a terracotta pot opposite the bench, its shiny leaves lit by a floodlight from the wall above.

115

He turned to look directly at Nadia, his eyes burning with fierce intensity.

'Now that *is* a good question. You said you wanted the truth. The truth is I married her for her money. I was literally starving. Well, not quite literally, but I couldn't sell a painting to save my life. Jan came along. Wanted a very unconventional lifestyle. Wanted an artist. I often think it wouldn't have mattered who; it was just good for her image, I think. I was available and quiescent. It was nice to be able to eat and I have to say the idea of having some of her friends join us in bed was not . . . unexciting. Now I don't need her money.'

'Or her?'

'That's the big question, isn't it? And I don't know the answer.'

'Don't you have to go home?' She hoped he would say yes. She needed to be alone.

'I do,' he said simply.

She couldn't sleep. Sweat ran off her body and she tossed and turned, unable to turn off her mind. It had only happened once. She'd forgotten about it. No, that was absurd. She hadn't forgotten about it at all. What she had done had been to build a wall around it, a thick, high, impregnable wall, water-proof, soundproof, memory-proof. It worked most of the time.

But as she had sat out in the garden with Hamilton, his words had brought it back so strongly, so graphically, it seemed it had happened just yesterday. The wall that kept it separate had preserved it, too.

It had been the summer, like now, hot and humid, making sleeping difficult. She could hear her voice.

'Are you awake?'

It was a huge Tudor house with countless bedrooms. She was eighteen. Her best friend at school had invited her to stay for the weekend. Her parents were rich. It was the summer before they would be parted to go to different universities.

'Yes.'

The huge, stripped oak floorboards creaked as Barbara slipped into the bed beside her. There was a full moon outside, the ghostly grey light streaming through gaps in the curtains. Barbara was upset.

'Did you see what Greg did to me?'

'He's a pig.' Greg had spent dinner ogling a friend of Barbara's mother and had taken her home in his MG instead of staying the night. Greg was supposed to be devoted to Barbara.

'Oh Nad, I can't stand it.' She started to cry, wrenching, convulsive sobs.

Nadia put her arm around her for comfort.

'All men are pigs,' she said.

'Pigs,' Barbara agreed.

As the weeping subsided gradually Barbara nestled her face to Nadia's neck. She began kissing her. It seemed a natural thing to do. She kissed her cheeks and then her mouth, but only little, pecking, affectionate kisses. Her hand slipped on to Nadia's breasts, pushing against them gently. She untied the ribbon that held the neck of her broderie anglaise cotton nightdress together.

'What are you doing?' Nadia said, only then feeling any alarm.

'I need it, Nad,' Barbara whispered into her ear. Her hand became more insistent, kneading Nadia's flesh, pinching at her nipples. She stripped back the top sheet, and before Nadia really had any idea what she was going to do, prised her thighs apart, and planted her hand over her sex.

'Oh Babs . . .' Nadia said, caught between wanting to push her away and wanting more of the delicious feelings Barbara's fingers were producing.

'I need it, Nad,' Barbara repeated. She trailed her mouth down Nadia's body and in seconds it was on her sex, her tongue circling Nadia's clitoris. It was the first time she had ever felt a mouth, any mouth, down there. The combination of heat and wetness created a wave of feeling she didn't understand but wallowed in. 'Do me,' Barbara said. 'Please Nad, do me.'

Barbara swung her thigh over Nadia's face and pulled up her nightgown until it was around her waist. Slowly she lowered her sex on to Nadia's mouth. Nadia remembered exactly how it had felt, hot and incredibly soft, and molten inside. She knew they shouldn't be doing this, that it was wrong, but the guilt seemed to make the pleasure sweeter. What Barbara did to her she mimicked on Barbara. *Soixante-neuf* – they had giggled about it in French class. It felt so good, so real, so comforting. They shuddered and trembled and rocked together on the bed, and came together too, with an intensity Nadia had never experienced before.

She had never wanted to see Barbara again. They had not mentioned what had happened the following day and Nadia refused all Barbara's subsequent invitations, until, eventually, Barbara had taken the hint and stopped asking.

But she had never experienced pleasure like it. Until now. Until Hamilton.

Nadia tossed and turned, unable to get comfortable, too hot with a single sheet covering her, too cold without it.

Every time she closed her eyes she saw an image of Jan Hamilton. She was lying propped up against the pillows of the bed in the studio, her long legs crossed, her dark eyes containing a question. It was not a question Nadia wanted to answer.

Chapter Six

STRIKE WHILE THE iron is hot. Was that what he was doing? He'd called her at work. They'd only picked at the food last night. Why didn't she bring what was left over to the studio? They could finish it off. Waste not want not, he'd said. And he wanted a lot of her. They could spend the night together. His wife was off on a shoot for a magazine.

She'd agreed.

He told her he had to go to a gallery first. There was a key hidden under the third step on the exterior stairs where a piece of concrete had worked loose. She could let herself in.

She had.

It felt strange to be in his studio alone. She prowled around looking for evidence, though of what crime she did not know. She was glad he'd called. She wanted to see him again, there was no question of that. The fact that his revelations had stirred such memories was nothing to do with him, or what she felt for him. She had made her decision and she was going to stick by it. A time would come, inevitably, when the advantages of passion were outweighed by the disadvantages of the lies and deceits it involved. But that time was not yet.

Nadia was firmly in control of herself. She knew what she was doing and why. As for the wall around her memory of Barbara, that could be rebuilt brick by brick. Or perhaps it didn't need to be. It was years ago. It had definitely been a trauma in her life and she had hidden it away for fear it meant more than she cared to admit. But now she knew herself better and the fear seemed faintly ridiculous.

He'd told her he'd be there at eight. She'd put the food in the kitchen and a bottle of red wine on the work surface. At ten to eight she stripped off all her clothes and lay naked on the bed. The studio was hot and she did not cover herself. It was exciting. Her nipples were hard and corrugated. She opened her legs wide and bent her knees as if to practise what she would do when he arrived. She could not resist the temptation to touch herself and found her clitoris was as hard as her nipples. She heard his footsteps on the stairs outside.

It was all like a dream from then on.

He opened the front door. Seeing her on the bed he came over and stood looking at her. She did not close her legs. She wanted him to look at her. She knew she was wet. She hoped he could see that. He looked at her intently, examining every detail of her sex, the deckled outer labia, the scarlet oval that was the gate to her vagina.

He pulled off shoes, trousers, shirt, dropping them on the floor, his cock emerging from his clothes already erect. He leapt on her, covering her, his strength pushing down against her, the hard muscle of his body a perfect match for the hardness of his cock. In seconds they were joined and his cock stabbed into the depths of her, filling her completely, a rod of hot steel her body clung to compulsively. Her first orgasm came so quickly it was almost painful, forced out of her before she had time to catch her breath.

They rolled and writhed on the bed, each desperate to give the other pleasure, each finding reasons to take their own. Hamilton was relentless. He hammered into her body, prising it open like an oyster to get at its soft, defenceless heart. She lost count of how many times she was racked with pleasure, her nerves stretched out like the strings of a harp, thrumming in harmony. Unashamedly she ground her clitoris against the base of his phallus, rocking her hips from side to side, revelling in the feeling of being penetrated so comprehensively.

It was entirely possible that they came together. Since she could hardly remember a second when she was not coming or beginning to come again, his orgasm must have overlapped with hers. She felt him slow, make space for himself in the cavern of her sex, and spasm, his cock kicking against the tight confines of the sheath that surrounded it. But by that time Nadia was too high, too intoxicated by passion, to separate these feelings from the general melange of pleasure she was already experiencing.

Eventually, exhausted, they rested. Nadia brought chicken and salad to the bed and they ate and drank the red wine, picnicking on the tousled sheet, their eyes never leaving each other's naked bodies, their arousal still not flagging, the food hardly tasted at all, just necessary as fuel.

'I've never wanted a woman more than I want you,' he said.

'I've never wanted a man more either,' she

replied. At least she thought that was what they had said. Later she could hardly remember any words being exchanged. She knew she *had* never wanted a man more. No man had ever made her feel what Hamilton made her feel. No man had ever reached down into the secret mechanisms of her libido and found the switches and levers that controlled it. No man had turned every gesture, of hand and mouth and eye, into a eulogy of sex, a secret, private oratory to some sensual god.

She did remember what they had done after that. She'd taken the food back to the kitchen. She'd glanced at the painting on the easel which for some reason she had not registered when she'd been alone. One of the shadowy figures in the foreground had been filled in, a striking, rather masculine woman, her hair and dark complexion suggesting Pre-Raphaelite influences. The other figure, though now clearly a woman, remained obscure. Her head had been painted but not her face.

Hamilton lay on the bed watching her as she stood by the easel. 'Come back,' he said.

And then it was as though they had never been parted. He pulled her down on to the bed, lay her on her back and began kissing her body, running his lips over her breasts, sucking her nipples into his mouth, moving down between her legs, finding her swollen, eager clitoris and renewing all the feelings that had swept over her before.

She spread her legs wide apart, allowing him to tongue the whole plane of her sex. He pushed his fingers inside her, creating a jolt of pleasure that made her gasp. Licking her labia from top to bottom first, he narrowed his attentions to her clitoris, circling it with the tip of his tongue, prodding it, provoking it, causing her eyes to close as she wallowed in sensation. In the darkness she felt the beginning of an orgasm throbbing in her body like an engine. That was why she hadn't seen her, of course, but she would never be able to understand why she hadn't heard her opening the front door or walking across the studio floor.

'He's good at that, isn't he?' she said.

It was so perfectly timed. Nadia opened her eyes but even the shock of seeing Jan Hamilton standing looking down at her could not stop the flood of orgasm as Jack's tongue swept, like a tiny brush, over her clitoris. In fact, she knew later, the way the woman's dark eyes had flicked approvingly over her naked body had sent her orgasm into overdrive. She writhed on the bed, the dark eyes following her, unable to do anything else.

'Well, quite a performance,' she said as soon as Nadia was still.

Jan Hamilton was, if anything, more beautiful than the hundreds of photographs of her suggested. She was tall and slim, with long black hair that shone with health. Her Mediterranean complexion made her very regular teeth in the large but thin mouth seem translucently white. Her face was striking, the angular contours of her brow, cheeks and chin giving her an air of severity that was counterbalanced by the warmth and brightness of her dark brown eyes.

She was wearing tight Lycra leggings in pure white, and black thigh boots folded over above the knee like a pirate. The leggings were so tight they had dimpled into the crease of her sex. Her black blouse, a blouson design, was made from chiffon with very full sleeves. Nadia could see her white lacy bra underneath.

'I got your note,' she said to Jack.

Hamilton raised his head as his wife sat on the bed. She took his cheek in one hand and kissed him, deliberately letting Nadia see her tongue lap up the wetness that clung to his lips.

'Mmm . . . Tastes good,' she said, looking at Nadia.

It was at that moment that Nadia had to make a decision because it was then that Jan stretched out her hand, the hand that had held her husband's cheek, to touch Nadia's breast. As if in slow motion Nadia saw it moving towards her, feet, then inches, then a hair's breadth. Her mind was in turmoil. She did not know what to think or do. But she did know that if those long, beautifully manicured fingers, their nails varnished a deep dark red, touched her she would have no control.

She had seen a movie once where a woman had died. Her spirit, in the shape of a white image of her body, had peeled away from her supine form, sat up, got up and walked away. That was exactly what she felt like now. She wanted to sit up, to push Jan Hamilton's hand away, to get to her feet and dress calmly but with dignity, and walk out of Hamilton's life forever. That was what her spirit wanted but it had no corporeality. Her body, on the other hand, was firmly rooted in more mundane realities, in the throes and thrills of passion and self-gratification. She was not dead, nor could she split herself in two.

Jan's hand cupped her firm round breast.

'No,' she said as a reflex.

'No?' Jan queried, smiling a knowing smile, as though she already knew Nadia's secrets. She did not take her hand away.

It felt as though the fingers that gently squeezed Nadia's pliant flesh were plugged into some source of electricity. Tingling shocks of sensation spread through her, over to her other breast, out through already over-wrought nerves. Her nipples, though rock hard, puckered further, the corrugations in the pink flesh cutting deeper, pimples on her areola forming in profusion. The electricity coursed down to her sex, her clitoris experiencing the same engorgement, swelling against the hood of her labia. Inside her vagina she felt the pulse that usually accompanied a flood of juices.

She should get up and walk away.

'You're quite lovely,' Jan said, trailing her hand from one breast to the other. In the world Nadia was inhabiting, a world turned on its head, where implications and consequences were suspended, up to now, she had made no commitment to what was happening. She had merely acquiesced. But now that changed. As Jan moved her mouth towards her lips, Nadia raised her head to meet it. She plunged her tongue into Jan's mouth and felt its softness, and heat. The kiss went on for a very long time. It sealed the silent contract she had made with herself. There was no turning back now, and no desire to do so.

Jan got to her feet. She stripped off her blouse and unzipped the boots. She peeled the tight leggings down to her ankles and sat on the bed to pull them off her feet. She was wearing white silk panties cut high on the hip.

Nadia looked across at Jack. For a second she thought she saw a flash of regret and resentment as if he didn't want his wife to be there. But it melted away. They both looked at Jan. Her body was flawless, every limb perfectly shaped, perfectly proportioned, smooth, seamless curves, rotundity and softness balanced by angularity and firmness, her whole body supple and lithe. She had a grace and economy of movement that matched her elegance.

Jan unclipped her bra and let her breasts fall free. They were small but very round with neat, dark red nipples. It was as Nadia watched them quiver slightly at their freedom that she felt the first pang of desire. She wanted to feel that long slender body pressed against her own, to feel her breasts and navel and sex, to do things she had only done once before, and had never thought to repeat.

They kissed again. Jan knelt at her side, Jack watching her intently. She trailed her mouth down the sinews of Nadia's neck, over her collarbone, down between her breasts. Nadia knew where the trail would end. She opened her legs as a way of telling the woman she did not mind, as if her whole body wasn't telling her that anyway, communicating with the language of need, her flesh trembling, her mouth mewing little gasps of pleasure.

Jan's tongue toyed with her soft, furry pubic hair. Slowly, as if deliberately teasing her, it descended lower, kissing the flesh on either side of her labia first. Then, after what seemed like forever, she centred her lips on the labia themselves. Nadia moaned loudly as Jan's tongue eased the yielding flesh apart and searched for the little bud hidden underneath. Jack's mouth had done exactly the same thing moments before but it was nothing like this. Jan's mouth was supple and smooth and incredibly soft. It seemed to mould itself to Nadia's sex, clinging to it limpet like, while her tongue

127

worked away inside, stroking at the clitoris. Strings of febrile memory stretched back to another place and another time, reinforcing the sensation.

As her mouth worked ceaselessly, Jan's hand slipped under Nadia's thighs. The fingers of one hand found the portal of her sex but instead of penetrating into her vagina they stretched it open, scissoring her fingers apart. At the same time Nadia felt a finger testing the ring of her anus. It had no difficulty penetrating the little puckered circle, the juices from Nadia's sex having collected there. As this finger pushed home the others thrust upwards, coming together to form a phallus in her vagina, mimicking the action of a cock – just as her husband's had once done.

As the fingers drove into both her passages, the tongue stroked harder at her clitoris. Nadia was torn between the exigencies of the shock of feeling Jan was creating and the vivid memory of what it been like before, of Barbara's tongue and mouth, the first time a mouth – let alone a woman's mouth – had touched her sex. She remembered the hot, sweet, almost sickly passion, mixed so strongly with guilt. Was knowing that it was wrong what made it feel so exquisitely right? Was that why she had exactly the same feeling now, her sexual passion mixed with the guilt of knowing she should not be allowing herself to take part in a *ménage à trois*?

Her eyes had been closed by the shocks of sensation. But she forced them open. She looked at Jan's slender body, her legs bent up under her, the silk panties stretched tightly over her buttocks. She looked up at Jack who was kneeling too, on the other side of her, his erection projecting from his loins. She tried to read the expression on his face. It

128

seemed, for a moment, to be anger.

Nadia was coming. A wave of sensation forced her eyes closed again and in the crimson darkness of her mind she saw images of Barbara, the forbidden memories fusing with the current feelings, until she could not tell one from the other. It didn't matter. All she cared about was the sweet, rich, dark pleasure that erupted inside her and spread out rapidly to every last nerve, wiping out the need to think, or do anything but feel.

A weight moved on the bed. She sensed the warmth of Jan's body. When her crisis had passed and she could open her eyes again she saw Jan was straddling her face, her legs open, her sex covered by the crotch of the silk panties. In the miasma of feeling her brain refused to work. She couldn't understand how Jan's fingers were still inside her yet at the same time peeling the crotch of the white panties aside, until she realised it was Jack's fingers moving the silk and that he had come to kneel behind her head. As he revealed Jan's sex he moved his erection towards it. Jan's labia were thin and neat, rather like her mouth, and, whether naturally or not, completely hairless. Nadia stared as they parted to welcome Jack's glans, just like a mouth pursing in a kiss.

Hamilton plunged forward, his cock disappearing into the maw of his wife's sex. Nadia's body pulsed over Jan's fingers. She had never seen anything like this and never realised how exciting she would find it, how her sex would react as if the cock were penetrating *her*.

Instantly she felt another orgasm spring up from the fathomless well of passion she appeared to have become. She had stopped struggling with her conflicting emotions. There was nothing she could do about it now anyway. This was not the time for moral judgments. This was not the place to sort past from present, nor tell herself what she should or should not be doing. At this moment it didn't matter. All that mattered was the glorious feeling of sex, the feeling she had missed for so long. There would be time for regret later, no doubt.

Clutching at the sheet, clawing at it with her hands in a desperate need to hold on to something, she came again, over Jan's artful tongue and adept fingers. She fought to keep her eyes open, knowing the view of Jack's cock sliding effortlessly into Jan's sex would only deepen what she felt.

Recovering slightly, Nadia raised her head off the bed, pushing her mouth up against Jack's cock. She saw him shudder as her lips sucked at the underside of his phallus.

'Oh God,' he groaned.

Nadia tasted the sap of Jan's body. Though it was years ago she could still remember the taste of Barbara's sex, just like this, sweet yet salty at the same time. The breadth of Jack's cock had spread Jan's labia wide apart and Nadia could see the little nut of her clitoris, pink and swollen and glistening wet. Inching forward she brought her tongue on to it, her chin butting against the sac of Jack's balls.

As a reaction she felt Jan's tongue go rigid. Aggressively, using the same motion Jan had employed on her, she prodded and stroked her clitoris, making her moan.

It was too much for Jack. Nadia's hot breath and the movement of her lips was making him come and he didn't want that, not yet at least. He pulled out and shifted around to the side so he could watch.

130

With her husband gone Jan could sink herself more fully on to Nadia's mouth, and Nadia, in turn, had access to her lower labia. Nadia moved her hands round Jan's buttocks using one to pull the crotch of her panties aside, as Jack had done, so she could get her tongue into her vagina. She circled the entrance first, then plunged inside. She lapped there for a moment before pulling back to Jan's clitoris and pushing the fingers of her other hand where her tongue had been, one into the small ring of Jan's anus, two into the heat and wetness of her sex.

It was a perfect circle. As Nadia's tongue stroked the swollen gland of Jan's clitoris, her own was similarly assailed. As she felt Jan's body tense and knew an orgasm was about to strike, so her own pleasure gathered with renewed force. Together the two women quivered and shook, their feelings mirror images, their bodies pressed together, every sensation magnified and multiplied by the fact that what one felt was instantly transmitted to the other like an echo trapped in a mountainous canyon, bouncing from one wall to the other, seemingly without end.

Finally the echo died; the shackles of passion that held them so tightly loosened their grip. Jan rolled off Nadia. They lay side by side, wet with sweat and their own juices, finally replete.

But there was still Jack. He was kneeling up on the bed, his erection glistening and hard, its veins standing out like cords of string, distended by his need. He moved up the bed until his cock was lying across his wife's lips.

'Feeling left out, are you?' she mocked, letting the words move her lips against his flesh. She sucked on the underside of his cock then squirmed back until her head was forced between his thighs and her flawless, lithe body lay out in front of him. She locked her lips around the sac of his balls and sucked it into her mouth. At the same time she circled the shaft of his cock with her right hand and began pumping the ring of her thumb and forefinger up and down, concentrating on the ridge of his glands.

Nadia watched. She saw Jack's eyes close as Jan's ministrations caused a jolt of pleasure. Not wanting to be left out of the final denouement, Nadia got up on to her knees. Crawling behind him she pushed her breasts against his back and sunk her mouth into his neck. At the same time she found his nipples and pinched them quite hard. He shuddered, driven that much closer to his climax.

Jan released his balls from their toothsome prison and juggled them instead with her tongue, the rhythm of her head incessant. Over his shoulder Nadia saw the head of his glans swell to even greater proportions, glistening and smooth, and the slit of his urethra open, like a tiny pleading mouth. Almost immediately a string of semen shot out of him, describing an arch in the air, and splashing down on Jan's trembling breasts and her belly and even, one or two drops at least, on the white silk of her panties that still veiled her sex.

She unlocked her car and sat in it without starting the engine. The interior of the car was familiar and comfortable. Eventually she drove home, concentrating on her driving, doing it with clipped precision, priding herself on the way she handled the sporty car, the way she cornered and positioned

132

it on the road. It was a means of distracting herself from thinking about anything else. There was little traffic and she watched intently for signs of the police as she drove well above the legal limit. She played a tape of Itzhak Perlman performing a Bach solo violin partita, playing it so loud the sound almost hurt.

At home she went straight to the bathroom, stripped off her clothes and stepped into the shower. She avoided looking in the mirror. She soaped herself vigorously then let the water wash the lather away.

She was exhausted physically and emotionally. She towelled herself dry and went to bed, covering herself with a single sheet. She knew she would not be able to sleep, that now, with nothing to distract her from her thoughts, nor the images that played in her mind, like pictures on a cinema screen, she would toss and turn, plagued by implications and consequence. Strangely she fell asleep almost before her head had touched the pillow.

On another day she might have thought twice. But not today.

'Hello?' She hoped it wasn't Hamilton. She couldn't remember whether she'd given him her home number.

'Can I speak to Nadia Irving?'

'You are.'

'Oh, hello, it's Andrew Anderson.'

'Mr Anderson, how are you? How did you get my number?'

'I know it's an imposition. I'm afraid I badgered James Hill.'

'That's all right,' Nadia said.

'I'd have waited to catch you at work but it was rather urgent.'

'Oh . . .'

She hoped nothing had gone wrong with her grand scheme.

'Not business,' he added, obviously picking up her anxiety. 'Purely pleasure.' He realised that sounded wrong and corrected himself. 'I mean I wanted to ask you out.'

'That urgent?' she said rather sharply.

Angela was sitting on the large cream Chesterfield in Nadia's first-floor sitting room, a glass of gin and tonic in her hand. She swirled the ice in the glass and mouthed, ''Who is it?'' to her friend.

Nadia mouthed back, ''Anderson''.

Angela made a ring of her thumb and forefinger and pumped her fist up and down. Nadia ignored her and turned her back.

'Well, it's just I've got tickets for the first night of the new Stoppard at the National. I remember you said at lunch you were mad about Antony Sher.'

'I am.'

'So I thought you might like to come. They say the rest of the run's sold out. But it's tomorrow night, you see, I thought you might be . . .'

'Tomorrow's fine and I'd love to come.' She wasn't sure she'd love to at all – Andrew Anderson was distinctly not her type and held little fascination for her – but she certainly wanted to see the play and she certainly did not want to stay at home on her own.

'Six then,' he said.

'That's early.'

'Starts at seven. Press nights are always early.'

'Six then.' It wasn't a problem. Working in the city

she started early but finished by five.

'Wonderful. I'll come and pick you up.'

'That would be nice.' She gave him her address.

'And dinner afterwards?' he asked tentatively.

'Can we take it one step at a time?' she said, not wanting Andrew to get the idea that he was to be anything other than a convenient companion.

'Of course,' he said.

They exchanged goodbyes and rang off.

'Andrew Anderson's got the hots for you, eh?' Angela guessed as Nadia sat down opposite her on a matching Chesterfield.

'So it appears. Wants to take me to the National.'

'Well, you could do worse.'

'It's the theatre, not a proposal of marriage.'

'He's single and rich.'

'And I'm not the slightest bit interested in him, Angela. Other than as a client.'

'What's the matter with him?'

'Absolutely nothing, except I don't find him attractive.'

'Not like Jack Hamilton?'

Nadia got to her feet, took Angela's glass and her own and refilled them with gin and tonic. She dropped in ice from an ice bucket and set them on the large coffee table between the two sofas.

'No, not like Hamilton.'

'So, where were we?' Angela sipped her drink. 'You're in the studio . . .'

Nadia had called Angela first thing that morning, the morning after the night before, and told her she needed to talk. Angela, perhaps hearing a note of distress in her friend's voice, had volunteered to come round that evening. For the last hour Nadia had poured out the whole story, everything that

135

had happened with Jack since she'd first met him. She'd got to the part where she had arrived at the studio on her own when Anderson's call had interrupted the flow.

'Can I ask you something really personal, Angela? I mean, we've been friends for a long time but we've never discussed it.'

'Discussed what?'

'Have you ever . . .' Nadia wasn't sure how to phrase it. She was going to say "made love to a woman" but that didn't sound right. "Have you ever had sex with a woman?" sounded wrong too. She settled for the familiar euphemism. 'Have you ever been to bed with a woman?'

'God, no,' Angela said rather too quickly. Nadia knew her too well. She knew immediately she was lying.

'Then you're going to be shocked.'

'Shock me.'

And she did. Angela's mouth fell open as Nadia related the rest of the story, telling her how Jan had let herself into the studio, and what had happened on Hamilton's bed.

'I only remembered what she'd said this morning. She thanked him for the note. She was supposed to be off on a photographic shoot, but he must have left her a note telling her about me. It was all planned. Like the others.'

'Others?'

'He told me they'd shared women before.'

'His wife's a dike?'

'Bisexual. That's the trouble.'

'What is?'

'I think I am too.'

'What, bisexual or a dike?' Angela tried to make a

joke of it.

'It's not funny. I enjoyed it, Angela, I mean really.'

'What's wrong with that?'

'Nothing, I suppose. It's just confusing.'

'You said Hamilton's had a terrific effect on you, got you all pumped up. It was probably just that you got so turned on she was like an extension of him.'

'Maybe.' She hadn't told her about Barbara, and the sticky sweet feeling that memory had provoked.

'Actually . . .' Angela said, her tongue between her teeth, 'I lied.'

'About what?' Nadia said as if she hadn't guessed.

'I have been to bed with a woman.'

'Recently?'

'You're right, we've never talked about it, have we?'

'We don't have to now if you'd rather . . .'

'Actually, I've been to bed with several women if you want the truth. Jan Hamilton was your first?'

'First *woman*.'

'Explain?'

'At school. Well, between school and university.' Nadia told her about Barbara. It was turning into a night of true confessions.

'Oh, my first experience was much more menial,' Angela said when Nadia had finished. 'It was when I was at Drew's. You remember my boss, the head of the bond department? Well, his wife propositioned me at the Christmas party. She knew I was up for promotion. She told me she was going to tell her husband she thought I was unsuitable.'

'And what? You didn't complain?'

'What could I do? Her word against mine. Nobody would have believed me. But that wasn't the point. I suppose that's why I've never talked

137

about it with you. You know the way I am with men? I love having sex with a man, with lots of men. I didn't have any idea I wanted to do it with a woman too, not until this woman came along. But I wanted her. She was beautiful. Oh, ten, maybe even fifteen years older than me, but she was gorgeous. Really long blonde hair, very slim with fabulous clothes. She always wore Joy 1000. It's supposed to be the most expensive perfume in the world.'

'And?' Their third, or was it their fourth, gin and tonic had disappeared. Nadia refreshed their glasses.

'She was very experienced. Very . . . adept. She knew all the right buttons to push. Oh, I was ripe for the picking but she was just so damn good at it.'

'And after her?'

'After her I have been very discriminating. The point of my telling you all this is that it hasn't made one iota of difference to my relationship with men. Never has and never will. That's what's worrying you, isn't it?'

'Yes, I suppose that's exactly what's worrying me.'

'I felt the same. I wanted it, I was desperately curious, but I was shit scared. I didn't want to turn into some bra-burning dike with a moustache, greased back hair and a man's suit. But it doesn't work that way. You know I love sex with men. I love it. Having sex with a woman is different, but in a way it's exactly the same. The pleasure comes from the same thing. I doesn't make you a bad person. In fact, as far as I'm concerned it makes sex better – the contrast, I mean.'

'Variety's the spice of life?'

'Right.'

'Why did you lie just now?'

Angela laughed. 'Well, firstly because I wasn't sure

what you were going to say and secondly because . . .' She reached into her handbag and took out a long, narrow parcel wrapped in red wrapping paper. 'After our last conversation I bought you a present and I didn't want you to take it the wrong way.'

Angela handed Nadia the package. 'The wrong way?' Nadia said.

'Open it.'

Nadia peeled off the red paper. On the inside she discovered a long yellow rectangular box with a transparent plastic window along part of one side and lettering that declared it contained a DREAM LOVER, THE ULTIMATE VIBRATOR (BATTERIES NOT INCLUDED). Fascinated, she extracted a cream plastic phallus from the box.

'I put batteries in,' Angela said.

'Where did you get it?'

'They have them all over the place. Twist the end.'

Nadia saw a gnarled knob at the end of the dildo. She turned it and the whole stem started to vibrate. She turned it off quickly because the action transmitted a jolt of sensation through her hand to her sex.

'You use one of these?'

'It's better than some of the men I've had.'

'What do you do?'

'Put it inside you. Put the end on your clit. Anything. You don't need instructions. Whatever's good.'

'And it makes you come?' Whether it was the drink or the subject of the conversation Nadia wasn't sure, but she was becoming very hot. She also thought she was blushing. She couldn't remember the last time she'd blushed.

139

'So, you see, I didn't want you to think I had an ulterior motive.'

'Ulterior motive?' The gin had affected her brain. She knew Angela had said the present might be misinterpreted, but, for the life of her she couldn't remember why.

'If I suddenly told you I'd been having sex with other women, then produced a vibrator, you might think . . .'

'Oh right.' The penny dropped. 'But you don't?' That remark slipped out before she realised what she'd said.

'Don't what?'

'Want to have sex with me?'

There was a silence. The words seemed to sober both women up.

'I think that would probably spoil a very good friendship,' Angela said earnestly.

'Probably?' Nadia queried.

'Yes.' Angela stared at her intensely.

'Meaning if it wouldn't spoil our friendship . . .' The words hung in the air. Both women realised they had taken a step on to territory they had never explored before.

'Let's talk about it another time. What are you going to do about Hamilton?'

'Nothing. I can't see him again.'

'Why not?'

'Oh Angela, I'm not like you. I scared myself. I scared myself badly. I should have got up and walked out.'

'Has he called you?'

'Twice. I got my secretary to say I was out.'

'But I thought you had a good time with him. In bed, I mean.'

'I do. I did. But I'm not going to become part of their *ménage.* I was used. He set me up for his wife. I know he did.'

'And if it were just him on his own?'

'Damn him. Why did he have to do it? I've never wanted a man more in my life. Christ, you don't know what it was like.'

'What do you mean?'

'Well,' the gin was making her loquacious, 'I was never very good at it. Sex, I mean. I never seemed to be able to get the hang of it. I thought it was me – that I wasn't very proficient. Then with him I went wild, really wild. Now I'm a different person. It's like I was asleep and he's woken me up.'

'I'd love to go to bed with him. I think he's so sexy.'

'He is.'

'So why don't you *use* him? As long as you know you're doing it. Men use women for sex all the time.'

'I just can't. I wish I could.'

'I've got to go,' Angela said, looking at her watch. 'I'll leave you to practise.'

'Practise?'

Angela indicated the dildo. For the second time that evening Nadia blushed.

'I'll call you a taxi.'

They chatted amiably while they waited for the taxi to arrive. At the front door they kissed each other on the cheeks.

'Thanks, Angela, you always seem to have the habit of saying just what I want to hear.'

'If you begin growing a moustache then you can start to worry.'

'Thanks for understanding.'

'I understand only too well.'

And that, Nadia had been surprised to discover, was undoubtedly true.

When she woke it was just getting light, fingers of light creeping around the gaps in the curtains, the room suffused with an odd cream tint. She was still wearing her bra and panties. The alcohol she had consumed with Angela had left her too tired to be bothered to strip them off.

She glanced at the clock on her bedside table. It was six-thirty. Next to it was a long rectangular box which she didn't recognise, until, all at once, it came flooding back to her, the gin-soaked confessions and Angela's gift.

She reached out and extracted the plastic cylinder from its wrapping. It felt cold and hard. There was enough light filtering through the curtains to see it quite clearly. The top was tapered and smooth, but two thirds of the length was moulded with little ribs circling its circumference. She was about to put it back when she felt her sex pulse, as though to remind her that, after a period of getting considerable attention, so far in the last twenty-four hours it had got none.

She stroked her pubic hair through the silky nylon of her panties, thinking she would go back to sleep. But her clitoris responded immediately. She could feel it swelling. And suddenly sleep was no longer on the agenda. Quickly, a little annoyed with herself for having started the process, she slipped out of her knickers, throwing the sheet that covered her aside. Remembering what Angela had said she trailed the dildo down her body until the tip was resting on the top of her thigh. Again she was aware of its coldness, in such contrast to the heat and life of a cock.

Without raising her head to look she groped around for the gnarled knob at the end of the phallus and turned it. A high-pitched humming noise filled the air and she felt her thigh vibrate. The vibration spread out like waves on a pond, and reached her labia. She experienced a delicious tingling sensation.

Nosing the dildo closer to her sex, she opened her legs. With one hand she pulled her breast uncomfortably from the silky nylon cup of her bra, squashing it down against her ribs, while, with the other, she directed the dildo into her labia. The vibrations extended all the way along the crease of her sex, affecting her clitoris too, but she didn't want to concentrate on that just yet. She wanted to feel it inside her. Slowly she moved the smooth cream plastic down to the entrance to her vagina. She remembered how Jan's fingers had stretched the opening apart, and used the tip of the dildo to do the same, circling it and pulling the pliant flesh this way and that. She felt a strong pulse of pleasure.

'Come on then,' she said aloud. Words seemed to have become an aphrodisiac.

She plunged the dildo home, right up into her body, objective experiment giving way to raw need. Her sex reacted to the intruder by going into spasm, contracting around it, gripping it tightly to feel its hardness.

'God,' Nadia gasped.

What Hamilton had done to her body, whatever process of atrophy he had arrested, seemed to override the guilts and confusions of being with his wife. The sexuality Nadia had so recently seen blossom remained in flower. Her senses reeled under the assault of the vibrator humming deep inside her. Almost unconsciously she began moving the phallus up and down in imitation of a cock. She felt her sex flooding with her juices. The spindle of the dumbbell had satisfied a need but this was so much better. She could feel blood pumping into her clitoris as it sent out urgent messages, pleading with her to bring the vibrations closer, wanting to be at the epicentre of the shock wave, not on the outskirts.

Nadia knew moving the dildo to her clitoris would make her come. For a while it was possible to tease herself, to hold the demands of her clitoris at bay and enjoy the pleasures emanating from her vagina, as the phallus stroked in and out.

But the storm of orgasm gathered more rapidly then she would have thought possible. The vibrations made her tremble, made her flesh quake, her breasts and thighs and buttocks alive. The dildo, almost of its own accord, slipped from her body and moved up, parting her almost hairless labia until the tip of the cream phallus butted hard against the pink wet promontory of her clit. She gasped with the jolt of pleasure it produced. The vibrations engulfed it. The feelings were so intense it felt as though she had been punched, a raw shock of energy that took her into an orgasm quite unlike anything she had experienced before. At its centre were the endless vibrations, tendrils of sensation that reached into every nerve, her body arched off the bed like a bow, her legs wide open, her muscles as rigid as steel.

It was the first time she'd come since she'd come with Jan. But fortunately for Nadia the rush of pleasure was so intense that it blanketed her mind. She'd feared she would see Jan's face or the image of her body, her thin, hairless labia and the open maw of her sex. She'd feared she would not escape the vivid emotional impact the experience had left. But, as the trills of vibration carried her down into a trough of pleasure, there were no mental pictures to reinforce the sensation. Her orgasm, like its creator, was completely disembodied.

Chapter Seven

AT EXACTLY SIX the doorbell rang. Nadia was waiting in the kitchen. She was dressed in a slinky, tight, dark blue dress that clung to her bosom, waist and hips. Its skirt was short enough to reveal a great deal of her slim, contoured thighs, and its scoop neckline, similarly, showed off the ballooning curves of her breasts. She loved this dress. It was comfortable to wear and immensely flattering and she was in the right mood to flaunt herself. Ultra sheer, glossy black tights and dark blue high heels completed her outfit.

'You're very punctual,' she said as she opened the door.

'It was bred into me from an early age,' Andrew Anderson replied. He was wearing a beautifully tailored double-breasted evening suit and a black bow tie. His cummerbund was cherry red.

'Do you want a drink?'

'I'd love one but I think we'd better go. The traffic's terrible at this time of the day.'

'Fine.'

She quickly set the burglar alarm, picked up her

small evening bag, preceded him out of the house, locking the front door after them. Parked a little way down the street was a silver Mercedes 500SL.

'Gave the chauffeur the night off,' he said as he opened the passenger door for her.

They drove through the traffic, crossed Waterloo Bridge and parked in the underground car park of the National, talking all the way: a little about the fact that Anderson had helped Manson's to negotiate a contract for Babcock's son to take a seat on the Manson board and a lot about the theatre and plays they had seen. Anderson was knowledgeable and astute and Nadia was impressed with his cultural expertise.

The foyer was crowded with glitterati and Anderson seemed to know a lot of the people who milled around, introducing her to one or two as they sipped a glass of champagne. The critics, with their dowdy suits and weary expressions, kept to themselves and took their aisle seats only at the very last minute.

The play was entertaining, for which Nadia was grateful. She had had a busy day at work, with only a sandwich at her desk for lunch, but that was exactly what she'd wanted. She'd had no time to dwell on the whys and wherefores of Jack Hamilton and his beautiful wife. She had reached one very simple conclusion, despite what Angela had said, with very little internal debate. With or without his wife, she never wanted to see Jack Hamilton again. She had lived dangerously, well beyond the pale of anything she would have thought herself capable of. Well, like a child who had strayed too far from home, all she wanted to do now was run back to safety.

By the end of the play Nadia was completely absorbed in its complexities. She had managed not to think about Jack Hamilton for at least two hours.

On the way out in the crush of people she took Anderson's arm.

'Thank you,' she said, smiling at him.

'My pleasure.' He returned the smile. For a moment their eyes met. 'How would you like me to take you home?'

'No,' she said definitely. 'I would like you to take me to dinner.'

'I took the precaution of booking a table at the Connaught Grill Room, just in case.'

They drove through Whitehall and Pall Mall. Outside the hotel a doorman sprung to open each door of the car, then, as soon as they were out, valet parked it. Nadia discovered she was ravenous. They ordered quickly, barely glancing at the menu, opting for *coquilles au gratin*, and chateaubriand with *soufflé, aux pommes*, a speciality that few restaurants could afford the manpower to prepare. Anderson ordered Tattinger champagne and a Margaux.

As the evening progressed Nadia found she liked Andrew Anderson more than she had thought she would. He was attentive and interesting, and though she had been put off in the first place by his rather weak appearance, she found it grew on her. He was not an unattractive man.

'Have you ever been married?' he asked after the coquilles had arrived.

'Yes. You?'

'Yes. A bad divorce. All my fault.'

'Children?'

'No, thank God.'

'Me neither.'

'Shall we compare divorces?'

'Too depressing.'

'Would you mind if I told you I find you very attractive?'

'Thank you.' She had the impression he wanted to say something else. 'And?' she prompted.

'Oh, nothing . . . It's all so difficult – well, I find it difficult.'

'Difficult?'

'What used to be called the mating game. Men and women. I'm too old to call it dating. When you were young you were allowed to be gauche and green. Youth was the perfect excuse. At my age you're supposed to know everything, exactly what moves to make, what to say, what to do.'

'And?'

'And I know nothing. I feel completely lost.'

'What did you want to say?'

'I want to say I'm extremely attracted to you.'

'You said that already.' That came out more churlishly than she'd intended.

'You see, I'm getting it all wrong . . .'

'Andrew . . .' It was the first time she had used his name. 'Perhaps I can make it easier for you. I've just been through a very bruising affair. I feel completely betrayed. I'm not ready; I'm not capable of going to bed with another man at the moment. When I am, if I am, I'll let you know.'

'That's very clear.'

'Sorry . . . I didn't mean . . . That area of my life's been very screwed up recently.'

'I understand. I appreciate your honesty.'

'Good. I'd like to do this again.' She wasn't sure whether that was true.

'So would I, very much.'

They ate the rest of the meal with gusto and ordered vanilla soufflé for dessert. The air had been cleared as far as Nadia was concerned and she could relax. Anderson, too, seemed to be more at ease having got the subject of sex off his chest.

It was well past midnight when they got back into the Mercedes and Anderson drove her home. He found a parking space almost outside her house and came round to the passenger door to open it for her.

'Well, good night, Nadia. I've really enjoyed your company.'

But Nadia found she didn't want the evening to end there. 'Come in for some coffee,' she said. It was Friday, after all, and she didn't have to be up at the crack of dawn.

'Are you sure?'

'Just coffee,' she said, smiling.

'That would be nice.'

Inside he stood in the kitchen while she filled the coffee maker and switched it on. She took out small white cups and saucers and set them on an oak butler's tray.

'Do you want a drink?'

'Better not,' he said. 'I don't think I should be driving as it is.'

She poured herself an Armagnac and put it on the tray. Upstairs Anderson settled on one Chesterfield and Nadia sat opposite on the other, the tray on the table between them.

'Do you want to talk about it?' he said, 'Or have you talked about it so much you're sick of the subject?'

'Talk about what?'

'Your bruising affair.'

She found she did want to talk about it. She leant forward, poured the coffee and pushed a cup across the table towards him.

'For the first time in my life I let myself go,' she told him. 'I took a risk, and lost.'

'What sort of risk?'

She looked across at Anderson. His neat, small face was serious and concerned. She couldn't help thinking of a small boy who had found his mother in tears and was trying to comfort her.

'I just wanted a man . . . I thought I was . . . what's the expression . . . past caring.'

'And he let you down?'

'Yes.'

'Did you love him?'

'No, curiously I can't say I did. I can't say I even cared for him very much.'

'Then why were you so upset?'

It was a good question. She wasn't sure she knew the answer. She hadn't felt love for Hamilton at any stage, though she knew love would be a natural development from what had happened between them. She supposed the reason she was upset by what had happened was that she felt used, that instead of responding to what she had thought was something special he had merely treated her as another affair, another prize to be shared with his wife.

'Because he used me,' she said after a pause.

'Used you how?'

'Do you want to know the truth?' She hadn't imagined telling Anderson such intimacies but she realised she didn't care enough about him to hide anything. If he was shocked and put off by it, she really didn't mind.

'If you want to tell me.'

'He shared me with his wife.'

She expected shocked horror. She expected him to ask when and how and why. Instead he said quietly, 'He must be a very arrogant man.'

Nadia laughed. 'Yes, you're absolutely right, he is.'

'And is that the sort of man you like?'

'What, arrogant? No, I don't think so.' She drank her brandy. Confession was good for the soul. The way Anderson had handled the news pleased her; it made her feel as though what she had done was not so beyond the bounds of acceptability after all. 'You're a very unusual man,' she told him.

'I take that as a compliment.'

'It is.' Nadia was looking at Andrew through different eyes. For the first time she wondered what it would be like to go to bed with him. The talk of Hamilton had inevitably put sex back on the agenda. 'Come and sit over here with me.'

Giving her an old-fashioned look, Hamilton got to his feet and came round the coffee table to sit beside her.

'Is that better?'

'Are you a gambling man?' she asked.

'No.'

'Oh, what a pity. I was going to offer you a gamble.' It was extraordinary. It was as though her body had changed gear. One minute she was calm, rational and objective. The next she felt a knot of anticipation cinch itself tightly in the pit of her stomach, and a wave of desire wash over her. She wasn't sure whether it was desire to have sex, or desire to have sex with Anderson. She knew it was desire to have sex with a *man*.

'What sort of gamble?' he asked.

'I was going to say that if you kissed me I might like it and if I liked it I might change my mind.'

'About what?'

'About what I said in the restaurant.' She was playing the vamp again. It appeared to be a role she enjoyed. 'On the other hand . . .' She smiled coquettishly. 'I might find the whole thing totally uninteresting and make you go home.'

'Quite a gamble.'

'But you're not a gambling man.'

He turned towards her, pushed her back against the Chesterfield and kissed her on the mouth. His tongue probed between her lips, but she pushed it aside with her own and penetrated his mouth. His hands caressed her shoulders very lightly. She felt her nipples pucker.

He sucked on her tongue gently then broke the kiss with an audible pop. 'Well?' he said.

Nadia got to her feet. The excitement she felt made her a little light-headed. She wasn't sure whether it was the kiss that had engendered it or the way she was acting. 'It pays to gamble, you see,' she said, extending her hand.

'You're very beautiful,' he said, taking her hand in both of his and rubbing her fingers very gently in a circular motion.

'Take me to bed, Anderson.'

'I thought you weren't ready?'

'I've changed my mind.'

Without another word she led him upstairs. In the doorway of her bedroom she turned and kissed him again, wrapping her arms around him under his jacket and pressing her body against his. She wasn't sure why she had suddenly been overcome by an urgent sexual need, apparently with no cause, but it had seized hold of her so strongly that her body was already tingling.

'The zip's at the back,' she said, turning her back to him.

'I noticed. It's a beautiful dress.' He caressed the material lovingly, smoothing his hands down on either side of her waist where the dress clung to her hour glass figure. 'Lovely material,' he said indistinctly, before pulling the tongue of the zip down. He folded the shoulder straps over her arms so the dress could fall to the floor. As Nadia stepped out of it he stooped to pick it up, and laid it carefully over the bedroom chair. Apparently not satisfied it was crease free, he shook it out and lay it across the chair a second time.

Nadia was wearing a black bra and matching panties under her tights. She stripped back the bedding, turned on the bedside lamp and drew the curtains. Taking a red scarf from a big mahogany chest of drawers, she draped it over the light. The bedroom was plunged into a rosy glow.

'You know, I was quite prepared to . . . I mean, you didn't have to . . .' Andrew said, taking off his jacket.

'I want to, Andrew. Women are allowed to want.'

She kissed him again. His hand found the catch of the lacy three-quarter cup bra and undid it. He pulled back from her mouth and eased the bra away from her breasts.

'Lovely,' he said. As he appeared to be paying more attention to the bra than to the breasts, Nadia wasn't sure whether he meant her or the garment. He put it on the chair, alongside her dress. 'Sit on the bed,' he said.

She did as she was told and he came to kneel in

front of her. Taking her left foot in his hand, he eased her shoe off. 'Such beautiful ankles,' he said, running his fingers around them. He bent his head forward until he could kiss the top of her foot. Then he took off her right shoe and kissed that foot in the same way. His hand smoothed against the glossy nylon.

Anderson got to his feet. He unbuttoned the gold studs that held his evening shirt and stripped it off. His chest was slender and hairless. He kicked his shoes off, peeled away his socks, reached behind him to unhook the cummerband, then unzipped his trousers. He was wearing shiny red silk boxer shorts. He was not as meticulous with his own clothes as he had been with Nadia's, merely leaving them where they fell on the floor.

Nadia lay back on the bed. She extended her foot and touched his thigh with her toes, working them up under the leg of the shorts. His legs, like his chest, were not defined by muscle, and were, oddly, completely devoid of hair. His body looked weaker and slimmer than it had looked in clothes, almost like the body of a young boy. She found herself comparing him with Hamilton. Damn Hamilton, she thought, consciously excising him from her mind.

'Help me with my tights,' she said.

Anderson knelt on the bed beside her and hooked his fingers into the waistband of the sheer nylon. Slowly he pulled them off her hips while she raised her buttocks. Instead of throwing them aside, he folded them as neatly as he could and laid them on the bedside chest.

The triangle of her lace panties barely covered her pubis. Strands of blonde pubic hair had meshed with the nylon. She was about to take them off herself.

'No, let me,' he said. His fingers caressed the lace, smoothing it against Nadia's mons. She saw him close his eyes momentarily as if to concentrate on the feel of it. 'Is it silk?' he asked.

'No, I don't think so,' she said, thinking it a strange question.

His hand slid down between her thighs, pushing the material into the crease of her sex. The gusset of the panties was made from a silky satin. As Nadia opened her legs he ran a finger along it.

'Take them off, Andrew,' she said.

With a certain reluctance his hands skimmed the panties down her hips. When they were clear of the ankles he brought them up to his face, rubbing them against his cheek. 'I'm sure they're silk,' he said, folding them carefully and putting them on top of her tights.

His hands cupped her firm, round breasts, squeezing them gently. He kissed her again on the mouth as his hand descended to her belly. A finger inveigled its way between her labia. Conscientiously he stroked the nub of her clitoris, while his mouth kissed her neck and worked down to her nipple. She felt his lips close on the hard puckered flesh and suck on it, covering it with saliva.

Nadia had the feeling he was making love to her by rote, as if he had read somewhere this was what a woman wanted, not because *he* wanted to do it. While she had been clothed his caresses had contained a certain electricity; now she was naked that spark had gone. She felt her excitement draining away. She wanted to be fucked; she wanted to be taken and possessed. Like Hamilton

156

had possessed her. Damn Hamilton. It was no good expecting every man to be like Hamilton. Tony had been like him, at least in strength and power, but he was more likely to be the exception than the rule. 'What do you want?' she said. She had the feeling Andrew wanted something he was not prepared to ask for.

'I want you,' he said.

She sat up, wrapped her arms around his neck and kissed him full on the mouth, moving her other hand down into the fly of the silk boxer shorts. Her hand closed on his cock. It was erect but only partially so. He was not circumcised and his foreskin still covered his glans. She pulled it back and he moaned against her mouth. Her finger rubbed the tender flesh of his glans and she felt it swell.

'Take your shorts off,' she said.

'Would you mind if I kept them on? I love the feel of silk.'

She answered by pushing him back on the bed. It was an odd request but it hardly mattered. His erection poked through the folds of red silk. She circled it with her fist and moved her head up and down. It was harder now and she could feel it pulsing.

'If you like silk . . .' She reached over to the bedside chest and caught hold of her panties. She dropped them on his chest and used them to caress his nipples. Instantly she felt his cock throb strongly in her hand. She brought the panties down to his erection and wrapped it in them. His cock jerked visibly, harder and bigger now.

'Oh Nadia, that's so lovely.'

'Good.'

There was a time when she would have settled for less, when she would have accepted a sexual encounter full of fudges and compromises. But not now. Her body demanded more. She wanted to excite Anderson because she wanted to excite herself. She swung her thigh over his hips and poised her sex above his prettily packaged phallus.

'You're really turning me on,' he said.

'Do they feel good?'

'Oh wonderful, so soft.'

'Smooth and silky?'

'Yes, yes . . .'

She pulled the panties away and nudged his glans into her labia, using it, at first, to prod at her clitoris. A wave of feeling swamped her, together with a sense of relief. This was not going to be like Hamilton but it appeared she had managed to resurrect her excitement. With Hamilton she had been out of control. Tonight, her pleasure was going to come from her own machinations.

She sunk her sex down on to Andrew's cock, wriggling her clitoris against his pubic bone. She could feel the shiny silk against her inner thighs.

'Feels good,' she said, squirming against it.

'I love it,' he said. His erection throbbed inside her. He extended his hands and ran them over the sides of his boxer shorts, caressing the silk as he bucked his hips to ram his cock into her more deeply.

'Yes,' she said to encourage him.

She leant forward, supporting herself on her left hand. With the panties in her right she brought them up to his cheek and rubbed them against it.

'You'll make me come,' he whispered.

'I want you to come.'

158

'Do you think I'm terrible?' His face looked anguished.

'No. Why should I think that?'

'For wanting this.'

'I like it.' It was partly true. The oddness of the experience was exciting.

'Do you like to be licked?' he asked, looking into her eyes.

'I love it.'

'Let me do that first.' It was a little cold, these premeditated negotiations in what was supposed to be the heat of passion, but better that, Nadia thought, than a quick fumble and an even quicker ejaculation. He appeared to care what she felt.

She swung off him, expecting him to sit up.

'No, come up here,' he said, wanting her to sit astride his shoulders. 'So I can see you.'

'Like this?' she said, kneeling above him, her legs wide open, her sex inches above his face, open and exposed.

'It's so beautiful, Nadia, like an orchid, a rare orchid.' His hands came up to her thighs and held her firmly. He looked at her for a long time, then pulled her down on to his mouth. The first touch made her shudder, his tongue prising open her labia and finding the portal of her sex. He circled it, provoking all the sensitive nerves concentrated around it, then pushed inside, straining his tongue against its tendons, to get as deep as he could.

He was very good. His tongue was strong and articulate. It caressed and dallied with every part of her sex, exploring every nook and cranny. He pushed it into her vagina, he stroked it against the long slit of her labia, he butted it against her swollen clitoris. His cock pulsed. Nadia had the strange impression it was like a ritual, an act of worship, an adoration at the altar of her femininity.

Whatever it was, he was making her come. After covering every inch of her pudendum he concentrated on the clitoris. He seemed to know exactly where the most sensitive nerves were sited. His tongue swept over them, dwelling just long enough to provoke, then moving on, round in a circle, to return again. With absolute regularity he completed his tiny circuit, each sweep making Nadia's body grate with pleasure, creating the incessant rhythms of orgasm. The tempo was relentless and monotonous and perfect. Each circuit produced a moan of pleasure from Nadia, each moan louder and louder. Her body was trembling, her breasts quivering so much they were slapping against each other, producing yet more sensation.

She found herself grinding down on him, wriggling her buttocks from side to side, wanting to feel her labia against the bones of his face, and her wetness all over it. But she did not disturb his rhythm. Inexorably his tongue circled the button of her clit, a little faster perhaps as he sensed she was approaching her climax. She moaned again, a continuous wailing now. A part of her mind thanked Hamilton for what he had done to her, another part cursing him as it fought to exclude his image from a causal relationship with her orgasm. She looked down at Anderson's slight body, his cock projecting from the folds of red silk, stained and damped by the sap from her body, trying to concentrate on that as the totem of her pleasure.

As her orgasm escaped, driving through her body with the power and energy it had so recently discovered, she tried to think of Anderson. But she could not. Her mind was too full, too crammed with images of Hamilton and, worse, of Hamilton's wife. As she heard the wailing sound of her own voice reach a crescendo, she quite unexpectedly saw the cream-coloured phallus being pushed between her legs. The hand that held it was not hers. In her mind's eye she saw the long, carefully manicured fingers of Angela Barrett.

'No, no, no,' she cried, shaking herself violently, trying to rid herself of the spectre that had so unexpectedly appeared at the feast, at the same time wringing every last ounce of feeling from the final throes of her climax.

She felt release from the rack of pleasure that had stretched every tendon in her body, but did not relax. She pulled herself off Anderson's mouth, swivelled round and slammed her body down on to his cock, with no subtlety or finesse.

'Your turn,' she said rather aggressively, riding up and down on him, making his cock slide to and fro inside her, feeling the wetness of her sex running, like a river, over the whole length of him.

'Lovely,' he said. But he didn't sound convinced. His cock was hard but it was not throbbing. He moved one hand around to his belly and stroked the silk of his boxer shorts. His head twisted to one side, looking for her panties. They were lying on the sheet. He stretched out his hand but could not quite reach them.

Nadia saw what he was trying to do. She pulled herself off him, grabbed the panties, then sunk back down on him again.

'This is what you want, isn't it?' she said, not moving now, just holding him deep inside her.

'Yes.' The anguished look had returned to his

face, as thought he were admitting to a mortal sin.

She rubbed the panties against her breasts. His eyes watched avariciously. The satin gusset felt cool against her super-heated body. She dropped the panties on to his chest then rubbed them against his nipples one after the other. His cock immediately jerked inside her.

'You want that, don't you?' She moved the panties up to his face.

'Yes.' His expression was a turmoil of emotion, caught between anguished shame and extreme pleasure.

Nadia stroked the panties against his cheek.

'They smell so lovely,' he said.

'I always keep my empty perfume bottles in my lingerie drawer,' she told him. His eyes seemed to note this information as though it were something he needed to remember.

'You're wonderful, Nadia.'

His cock was throbbing strongly. She ground her sex down on it and used her internal muscles to squeeze it. She moved the panties down to his lips. He kissed them, pursing his lips against the lace. Nadia pushed the material into his mouth and he sucked on it. She saw the whites of his eyes roll up in an expression of ecstasy and felt his cock spasm, spattering out his semen into the cavern of her sex.

Chapter Eight

'*PLEASE.*'

She did not reply. There was nothing she wanted to say to him.

'Pretty please . . .' he said, trying to charm her. It did not work.

'Look, Hamilton, I've told you. I'm not interested. Not under any circumstances.'

She was looking at the largest bouquet of long-stemmed red roses she had ever seen. They had been delivered a minute after she'd got home from the office, the van driver waiting outside. The note read: "You're wonderful. Andrew."

'Nadia, I need to talk to you,' Hamilton was saying. He'd called her three times over the weekend. The first time she'd put the phone down then set her answerphone to monitor her calls. He'd called her at the office four times during the day but her secretary had been there to intercept. She answered the phone as she got home, thinking it would be Andrew.

'There's nothing to talk about,' she said.

'But there is. You think I planned it, don't you?'

'You did.' That was a mistake. She should have just put the phone down.

'No, Nadia. I told you Jan was supposed to be away on a shoot.'

'It doesn't matter. You're married. I don't go out with married men. I was stupid to agree to it. I've only got myself to blame.'

'I can't talk over the phone.'

'Good, because I told you I have nothing to say.'

'Just a drink somewhere, anywhere, just for half an hour.'

'No. How many times have I got to say it? No. And please don't call me again.' She slammed the phone down, its bell tinkling at the impact.

It rang again instantly.

'Look, I told you . . .' she shouted, grabbing the receiver off the hook.

'Nadia?' It was Andrew Anderson.

'Oh hi . . . sorry, someone's been pestering me about double glazing.'

'Did you get the flowers?'

'There was no need.'

'There was every need.'

'They *are* beautiful.'

'I meant what I said, Nadia. I haven't been able to stop thinking about you.'

For different reasons, she was sure, Nadia had not been able to stop thinking about him either.

'I have to go to Rome on Saturday. I wondered if you'd like to come with me. We could make a weekend of it.'

'Rome?'

'Leave Friday night, back Sunday night.'

'Sounds lovely,' she said. The idea of a weekend in Rome, far from Jack Hamilton, was enticing. She wasn't at all sure what she felt about Anderson, but did that matter? He was pleasant company and, though he had been rather odd in bed, he had also been conscientious. And he had, as the Americans said, given very good head. She smiled at the thought.

'Does that mean you'll come?'

She hesitated a full half second. 'I'd love to.'

'Pick you up at six. There's an eight o'clock plane.'

Three days later she was parking her car outside her house. It was the first time all week she had come straight home from the office. There had been a reception at the American Embassy on Tuesday and a leaving party for one of the employees at Hill Brothers on Wednesday. She was relieved to have the whole of Thursday evening to pack for Rome.

She locked the car and extracted her house keys from her handbag.

'Nadia.' Jack Hamilton came up behind her as she walked towards her house. He must have been waiting for her out of sight round the corner, since she hadn't seen him as she drove up.

'What are you doing here?' She tried to sound angry but the wave of purely physical pleasure she experienced at seeing him again took her completely by surprise.

'I told you, I had to see you.'

'I've been busy.'

'I know. I've waited here every night.'

'Jack.' She tried to put aside the way her skin had turned to goose pimples and her heart raced. She tried to discount the fact that she was having to remember to breathe. 'Jack, I've got nothing to say to you.'

'Nadia, something happened between us, didn't it? Tell me honestly that you didn't feel something special and I'll go.'

'What do you mean?'

'For God's sake, Nadia,' he said angrily, attracting the attention of a woman walking a Yorkshire terrier on the other side of the road. 'You know what I mean.'

'You're married.'

'And if I wasn't?'

'You are. End of story.'

'If I got a divorce?'

Her heart was pounding so hard against her ribs she was surprised she couldn't see it bulging from her blouse. She wheeled round and stared at Hamilton. He was wearing his usual washed-out denim jeans, with a blue shirt and a white T-shirt underneath. His black hair hung down over his forehead, almost falling into his left eye. He brushed it aside with a characteristic shake of the head.

'You're not getting divorced. You're happily married, remember? I saw it for myself, Jack. You do everything together, you *share* everything.'

'I didn't plan that.'

She could feel sweat breaking out on her upper lip. The late afternoon sun was shining straight into her face. There seemed to be a buzzing in her ears as though some sort of flying insect was trapped there.

'I was there. You left her a note.'

A tubby little bald-headed man marched up the street with a determined stride. 'Excuse me,' he said as he walked between them.

Jack looked blank. 'A note?' he queried.

'A note, Jack. She said she'd got your note. Don't you remember? What did it say? I'm at the studio with a new girl, come right over?' Nadia stormed through her gate and up the path to her front door, her anger at last winning out against her other emotions.

'Nadia.' He charged after her and caught her by the arm. 'I left a note to say I'd gone to Manchester, just in case she got back early and thought of coming to the studio. She was being ironic.'

'Can't you do better than that? Leave me alone.'

Another passer-by, a young man in a black leather jacket, stared at Hamilton aggressively, then stopped at Nadia's gate.

'You all right, love?' he asked.

'Fine,' she replied, not wanting any interference. 'Just go,' she whispered to Jack. She put her keys in the door. The young man sauntered off.

'Nadia, this is ridiculous.'

It all happened at once. She opened the door and before she could stop him he had pushed inside and slammed the door behind her, pulling her into his arms and kissing her on the mouth. He crushed her against the hall wall, her breasts pressed against his chest, his erection engorging against her belly.

'Get out,' she spat, trying to free herself from his grip and tearing at his shirt.

'Nadia,' he gasped as she began raining blows down on his back. 'Can't you understand, I need you. I know you feel the same.'

He brought one hand up to her face, caught her by the cheek and forced his mouth against hers. She tried to squirm away but it was too late. Her body was already beginning to respond to Hamilton, the effect he had at a physical level overriding her rational response.

'No,' she said, tearing her mouth away.

'Yes,' he insisted, his hand twisting her back to face him, his mouth closing on hers. He had felt her body's reaction.

As his tongue plunged between her lips she felt her body channel the passion of anger into lust, hard, hot, throbbing lust. It took her by surprise with its intensity. Her hands, instead of clawing at his back like talons, held him tighter. Her sex pulsed. She kissed him back, pushing her tongue past his, vying for position in his mouth. Hungrily she tore his shirt out from the back of his jeans, wanting to feel his flesh. She had never wanted a man more in her life.

He was kissing her neck and her ears, his tongue hot and wet. His hand found the catch of her bra under the white cotton blouse she was wearing and snapped it free with dexterous, practised ease. He started to open the buttons at the front of the blouse, then, with frustration at the slowness of the process, grasped the two sides of the garment and ripped it apart, pulling her bra up to reveal her quivering breasts, their nipples already stone hard. His hands engulfed them, squeezing and squashing the firm orbs.

Nadia was fighting with his belt. She dropped to her knees, ripped his flies open and pulled his jeans and white boxer shorts down together. His cock sprung free and without any hesitation she took it greedily into her mouth, glorying in the feeling of its hardness and size. She took it right down her throat, sucking on it hard, and felt a response from her sex as though it were buried there too. He moaned as she sucked him again, not caring if she hurt him.

Seizing her by the shoulders, he forced her down on to the hall carpet, his cock plopping out of her mouth. She was wearing a cream linen skirt and white panties. He pulled the skirt up to her hips and caught the front of the panties in his hand, rucking up the material until the crotch was no more than a thin string. Pulling this to one side he forced himself between her legs and drove his cock into her labia. She was wet. On the tide of her juices his cock slid back easily, found the entrance to her vagina and, in one effortless moment, rammed into her.

For a second he did nothing, the haste and urgency that had gone before overtaken by blind pleasure, both of them wrapped in the same exquisite folds of feeling, animation suspended by ecstasy.

The second seemed to last forever, gathering in layers of emotion, febrilely connected to everything that had happened between them, every touch, kiss, caress, every deed and sensual perception.

It was ended by need. The rhythms of their bodies asserted themselves, pulling them back from the lofty spiritual plane to the grinding tempo of urgent desire. Nadia felt him begin to pound into her. She was uncomfortable, the floor hard and unyielding, her bra up around her neck, its wired cups digging into her throat, the thin string he had made of her panties cutting into her buttocks. But none of that mattered. All that mattered was the sword of flesh that invaded her, filled her, focused her every sense on her sex.

It was not a question of technique or size. What Hamilton did to her could not be explained rationally. His cock inside her simply *was*. It fused with her, as though he was not only inside her body but inside her mind. She knew she had started to come the moment he'd forced her back against the wall. Her sex had throbbed so strongly she knew he had felt it. By the time he was inside her the nerves of her body were knitted together in tight spasms, each one a stepping stone to the next, taking her higher and higher, as the hardness of his erection arched up into her. She could feel the velvety wet walls of her sex clinging to it. At the zenith of his stroke the neck of her womb seemed to open for him, like another tiny mouth pursed to welcome him.

'Jack, Jack . . .' Her hands clawed at his flesh under his shirt, her voice strangulated by passion. The back of her head was forced against the floor, at a right angle to her spine, the sinews of her neck stretched and prominent like cords of rope.

It was only seconds, only four or five strokes of his erection, and her orgasm was born, breaking over the crown of his cock, spreading out through her body so fast every nerve experienced the explosion at the same moment. Instinctively he did not pull out of her, but pushed his cock deeper instead, using all his considerable strength to thrust it further up, knowing this would reinforce her pleasure.

But there was more to come. Her orgasm was so long and detailed, each graduation in it separate and distinct, that it felt like a thing apart, able to grow and function independently. As Jack arched his cock into her, her orgasm rippled and bucked, seizing her body with a new wave of pleasure and taking her on to another plane.

'No, no, no . . .' she screamed. She was stretched out so tightly she thought she might snap. She wasn't sure she could take any more.

But she could. Her entire world had narrowed to

the tiny compass of her sex. Not even her whole sex, just the clinging niche at the top of her vagina, that gloved his glans. She could feel it minutely, every contour and line. It was throbbing. She knew he was going to come. He had crossed the invisible line between control and reflex. She knew he was going to jet his semen into her. She had never needed anything more desperately.

She could see, in her imagination, his glans, the smooth pink flesh glistening wet, the little mouth at its tip open and waiting. As she felt him spasm, jerking against the silky cell that imprisoned him, she was sure she could feel each jet of spunk splashing into her, each globule like a spark of life creating a new erogenous zone wherever it landed.

Did she come again or was her orgasm just propelled to new heights by those incredible feelings? Did it matter? All she knew was that her whole body was trembling uncontrollably, that she was moaning and tossing her head from side to side, that here, on her hall carpet, Hamilton, once again, had wrung feelings and sensations from her body she had never known it was capable of delivering.

At that moment an ear-splitting noise erupted in the hallway. Nadia's body reacted instinctively to the deafening cacophony of high-pitched sound, tensing as the adrenaline rushed through her. Her mind was so isolated from reality it took her seconds to realise its cause. She had forgotten to turn off the burglar alarm.

There was undoubtedly a tension in the air, an atmosphere that could be cut with a knife. Neither woman was relaxed, their body language tense and defensive, though both were equally determined, consciously at least, not to show it.

'Smells good,' Angela said. The weather had broken. After two weeks of heat and balmy evenings, a cold drizzle lashed at the French windows. Angela sat at the dining-room table watching Nadia putting the final touches to their dinner, in the kitchen. A big blue china bowl on the cherrywood dining table contained a green salad. Alongside it was a wooden cheese platter covered with a thick glass cloche, four French cheeses laid out underneath. There was a good bottle of burgundy already opened, a bottle of mineral water and two glasses at each plate setting.

Nadia brought in a white bowl of pasta with prosciutto, peas, shallots and cream. She divided it between two deep oval white plates and offered Angela freshly grated Parmesan cheese from a specially designed glass and stainless steel dispenser.

'So tell me about Rome?' Angela said.

'I didn't go.' Nadia poured the burgundy and tasted it.

'What . . . I thought . . .'

'I cancelled.' Nadia hadn't seen her friend since the night they had had too many gin and tonics. Angela had been away on a weekend residential course on the international futures market and had only spoken to Nadia briefly to tell her she would be away. At that point Rome with Andrew Anderson had been very much on the agenda.

'Why?'

'You have one guess.'

'Hamilton.'

'Got it in one.'

'Hamilton what?'

'Are you ready for this? He told me he wants to get a divorce.'

'A divorce!'

'Not entirely on my account. But he says I'm the catalyst that's made him realise his marriage is over.'

'When was this?'

'Thursday night. He was waiting for me when I got home. We spent the weekend together.'

'Jesus, Nadia, I had no idea. So, what, he's really serious about you?'

'He says so.'

'And what about you? How do you feel about him?'

Nadia didn't respond immediately. She wound her fork into the tagliatelle and took a large bite, then chewed thoughtfully while Angela watched her with mounting impatience. Finally, after a sip of wine, she put her friend out of her misery.

'I'm not sure yet. I've heard it all before, Angela. He was only with me this weekend because his wife was away in Poland working. I'm not kidding myself. When it comes to the crunch I have no idea what will happen. If he actually leaves her then it'll be a different matter. Until then . . . I'm keeping all my options open.'

'Including Anderson?'

'He's a nice man.'

'Nice? Nice is practically pejorative.'

'If I hadn't met Hamilton I think I could be really quite involved with him.'

'But?'

'There's something missing.'

'What?'

'I don't know.' Nadia knew precisely but wasn't

173

sure she wanted to broach the subject of sex. Sex was, she knew, the reason for the tension that laced the air.

Angela was less circumspect. 'He's not good in bed?'

'Yes. No. I don't know, I just get the feeling he wants something more . . . something else.'

'Mmm . . . Interesting. So what have you told him?'

'I lied. I told him I was going on a course about the international futures market.'

Angela laughed. 'Sounds familiar. But you can't put him off forever.'

'I suppose I'll have to tell him the truth.'

Angela chewed on the pasta. 'This is delicious. So what truth are you going to tell him?'

'That I've met someone else.'

'You think Hamilton's serious?'

'I haven't the slightest idea. But if he behaves himself, if he actually does what he says he's going to do . . . then who knows what might happen.' Nadia grinned broadly.

They changed the subject and talked about work as they ate salad and the cheese, then a pear and almond tart Nadia had made. She served it with chilled Beaumes de Venise.

'That was really great,' Angela said, finishing her second slice while Nadia put the coffee on. 'Can I have another glass of wine?'

'Help yourself. And pour me one.' The dessert wine was in a cooler on the table.

They took the wine and the coffee upstairs to the first-floor living room. Nadia realised, after she'd done it, that sitting on the same Chesterfield as her friend was a deliberate gesture.

'So what happens now?' Nadia said, emboldened by the wine – at least, that was her excuse. Hamilton had not only changed her sexual perceptions. It seemed he had also given her a hardiness she had never had before.

'Is something supposed to happen?' Angela replied, feigning innocence of the subject that was on both their minds.

'You tell me?' Angela's cautious response during their last conversation in this room hadn't killed Nadia's interest in the idea. Almost unconsciously, she had found herself thinking about what it would be like to have sex with her friend. The idea had slipped into her mind while she was with Anderson and had remained firmly lodged in her libido, resisting all her attempts to shake it free.

She looked at Angela with admiration, noting the way the one-piece tailored pants suit in a subtle beige suited her figure, how beautifully her red hair caught the light, and how her green eyes sparkled with life. She was not slow to realise it was not admiration she was feeling but desire.

'I thought we'd said it would be a bad idea.' There was no need to define what "it" was.

'You did.' Nadia picked up the glass of wine and sipped it. 'But now I'm not so sure.' She looked straight into Angela's eyes, wanting to see her reaction. There was no sign that she was shocked.

'You don't think it would spoil our friendship?'

'I'd like to try an experiment.'

'What sort of experiment?' Nadia thought she saw the expression in Angela's eyes change. They dropped to her bosom and seemed to be examining the cleavage that peeked out from the V-neck of her peach-coloured dress. She had tucked her legs up

175

on the sofa and saw Angela's eyes sweep over them, too.

'I told you I had an experience with a woman before Hamilton's wife. I tried to forget about it. It frightened me. I thought it was like a virus, that I'd become infected . . .'

'I know what you mean.'

'Then with Jan Hamilton, well . . .' She took another sip of the sweet golden wine.

'Well what?'

'With Jan Hamilton I could pretend I was doing it for Jack. I still don't know.'

'Know what?'

'If what you said is right – that it wouldn't take over my life.'

'It doesn't.'

'Because if it didn't I think it could be very pleasant. Very.'

'I don't want to lose you as a friend,' Angela said earnestly.

'You won't. That's too important.'

'Promise?'

'Cross my heart and hope to die.'

Angela got to her feet. She picked up her cup of coffee, finished it and looked down at her friend. 'Last chance to ask me to go,' she said.

'Stay,' Nadia said firmly, her pulse rate instantly racing.

'Give me five minutes then.'

Angela turned and walked to the door. Her footsteps mounted the stairs, then crossed the floor to the bedroom above, and went into the bathroom. Nadia felt remarkably calm. She had rehearsed what she was going to say and when she was going to say it and Angela had reacted exactly as she'd expected.

She had decided that it was time to get to know herself, to put an end to the uncertainties she had felt since she had been to bed with Jan Hamilton. The skeleton of Barbara had been hidden in her cupboard for too long. It was time it was out in the open, especially if she ended up making a commitment to Hamilton. That would involve forswearing *all* others.

Was that likely? Did she even want it? She did not know the answer to the first question but the answer to the second was very definitely, yes. No man had ever made her feel what Hamilton made her feel. She was in danger of admitting to herself, after their weekend together, that she could easily fall in love with him.

The five minutes had passed and there were no more footsteps echoing from the bedroom. Nadia finished her coffee, took a deep breath, and walked upstairs.

Her bedroom door was ajar. She walked inside and closed the door firmly behind her.

Angela was lying on the bed, her head propped up against the pillows, her ankles crossed, the triangle of pubes that nestled at the top of her thighs a mass of thick, unruly red hair. Her fingers were pressed together, as in an attitude of prayer, their tips resting against her bottom lip.

'Take your clothes off,' she said firmly. 'I don't want any fumbling.'

Nadia's breathing was shallow and her pulse continued to race. She had seen her friend naked before but the context had been different. Now she was looking at her as an object of sexual desire. Her body was beautiful, full and rich, plumper than her own, but not fat. Angela's body was a symphony of curves and cambers, the convexity of her breasts and hips and belly counterpointed by her long lithe legs and the narrowness of her waist.

'Where's the vibrator I gave you?' she asked. Nadia unzipped her dress. She slipped it off her shoulders and let it fall to the floor. She was wearing white panties and a matching bra.

'In the drawer.' She indicated the top drawer of one of the bedside chests.

As she unclipped her bra and shucked it from her shoulders she felt her nipples stiffen. Angela extracted the cream plastic phallus. She uncrossed her legs and opened them slightly, pushing the tip of the dildo into the crease of her labia, then closed her legs, trapping it so tightly it stuck up vertically from her thighs.

'Did you use this?' Angela asked.

'Yes.' Nadia pulled her panties down and stepped out of them. She picked up her dress and hung it on the back of the door. She left the panties on the floor, suddenly remembering the way Anderson had handled them.

'And?' Angela prompted.

Nadia sat on the edge of the bed. 'I never imagined it could affect me so much. Do you want to know the truth?'

'Yes.'

'I imagined you holding it in me.'

'Mmm . . . come here.' Angela took Nadia's arm and pulled her on to her side on the bed. Rolling on to her side too, the dildo still projecting from her thighs, she arranged herself in front of Nadia, their breasts touching, the base of the dildo brushing Nadia's pubic hair. They stared into each other's eyes, knowing it was the point of no return.

Angela leant forward and brushed her lips against her friend's without kissing her, as her hand cupped Nadia's breast. She squeezed it gently and moved it so the tips of their nipples were touching. Nadia felt a rush of pleasure out of all proportion to the caress. Her body shuddered. She pressed against the butt of the dildo.

'Open your legs,' Angela said. As Nadia did as she was told she felt the cold plastic slide against her labia, and Angela's thick pubic hair grazing her own. 'Turn it on, then close your legs tight.'

Nadia reached behind her back. The gnarled knob at the end of the vibrator was sticking out from the cleft of her buttocks. She turned it and the phallus began to vibrate strongly, its motor humming.

'Harder,' Angela said.

Nadia turned the knob to maximum and the vibration increased, the humming noise getting louder. She closed her legs and gasped as the vibrator was suddenly trapped against her sex. Her clitoris pulsed. Angela pushed her belly closer. It was fleshy and round in contrast to the flatness of Nadia's and felt wonderfully soft. Her pubic bone was hard, however, and Nadia could feel it grinding against her.

'Oh, it's good . . .' Nadia gasped.

'Yes . . .'

Angela wrapped her arms around her friend's waist and pulled her even closer. She brushed her lips against her face, kissing her cheeks and her chin and her throat, avoiding her mouth for fear that a full-blown kiss would turn her off. But Nadia had no such inhibitions. With both hands she held Angela's cheeks, staring at her intently for a moment, before she pulled their lips together and plunged her

179

tongue into Angela's mouth.

The kiss made her shudder, the pleasure from her sex arcing to join the heat and passion from her mouth. At once, as simply as if someone had thrown a switch, she felt her body falling towards orgasm, the ceaseless vibrations impossible to resist. As Angela sucked on her tongue, Nadia trembled like a feather in the wind, the feel of Angela's belly and breasts against her deepening the pleasure that exploded in her body.

'God,' she said, panting for air.

'How delicious, I felt you come.'

'Again . . .' Nadia said, feeling Angela pushing the vibrator forward as if it were a cock, so it was pressed even harder into Nadia's clitoris. A second orgasm, distinct and quite separate from the first, sprung through her. But this time she felt Angela's body tense too. Just as passion flooded over Nadia, she felt Angela's reaching fruition too. They clung together, both needing support, the feeling of their bodies pressed together adding to the pleasure. They quivered and shook and slid against each other until they could stand it no longer. Almost simultaneously they opened their legs and let the dildo roll on to the bed.

'Well,' Angela said. 'How's the experiment progressing?'

'I think I need more data before I can evaluate it properly,' Nadia replied, running her tongue against her friend's lips, before rolling on to her back.

Angela trailed her finger down Nadia's body until it reached her pubic hair. Nadia eased her legs apart and the finger continued downward until it was coated with the sticky juices from Nadia's sex.

Angela brought her finger to her mouth and sucked on it with an exaggerated gesture.

'So sweet,' she said, getting to her knees. She bent forward and kissed Nadia's breasts one after the other, then trailed her tongue along the same route her finger had taken.

Nadia felt the surge of excitement. 'Oh Angela,' she gasped as she felt hot breath against her sex.

'You want it, don't you.' It was a statement, not a question. Nadia's sex had angled itself towards Angela's mouth, her buttocks raised from the bed, her legs wide open. She could feel her clitoris throbbing and her wetness leaking from her vagina.

Angela stared at the rough-hewn folds of her friend's sex. Slowly, with the tips of the fingers of both hands she drew Nadia's labia apart so she could see the scarlet interior, glistening wet. The mouth of her vagina was open, the entrance an irregular oval, the cavern beyond an inky black. It seemed to be breathing, the deckled edges of the vertical mouth contracting regularly.

Dropping her lips full on to Nadia's sex, Angela kissed it as though it were a mouth, plunging her tongue into Nadia's vagina, lapping up her juices, and feeling Nadia's body clench with sheer pleasure. She licked from front to back, long licks using the whole width of her tongue, like a child licking an ice cream cone.

Nadia gasped, the shock of sensation mingling with a wave of affection for her friend. 'Together, ' she insisted, sitting up. For a moment the sight of Angela's head bobbing between her legs produced such a strong pulse of feeling it interrupted her purpose. 'Together,' she repeated when it had passed, pulling at Angela's leg.

181

Angela swung her leg over Nadia's shoulders, her sex open and poised above her friend's head. Her tongue began to concentrate on Nadia's clitoris, licking it with the very tip of her tongue, pushing it this way and that. Slowly she lowered herself on to Nadia's waiting mouth.

As Nadia watched the descent her body shuddered. Her excitement was intense. She didn't need to think about the implications and consequences of what she was doing. She had worried about destroying their friendship but the ability to give each other such intense pleasure was not going to be detrimental. It was like an affirmation of what they had always felt for each other.

Angela's sex was plump and hairy. As its softness pressed against her mouth, as she felt how wet she was, the sensual circle was complete. Nadia kissed the intimate flesh, her tongue separating the labia to find the nut of Angela's clitoris, ready to mimic what her friend was doing to her. Pushing it against the pubic bone, Nadia felt Angela do the same to her. The shock of sensation produced in one immediately translated to the other, amplifying the frequency of pleasure as it reverberated between them.

They wallowed in it. Nadia's orgasm blossomed in her body like a flower photographed by time lapse cameras, from bud to full-blown petals in seconds. But as it opened, as it spread through her it was communicated instantly to Angela by the flesh that was pressed against her, by Nadia's mouth, and tongue, and quivering breasts. The provocation tipped Angela over the edge too, orgasm seizing her just as surely and sending new shocks of feeling back to Nadia, exchanging everything they felt.

They shuddered and shook, coming together then separately, as one asserted an ascendancy, licking and sucking and nuzzling the soft, sweet flesh that melted over their mouths, contracting helplessly as it was moved by the tides of orgasm. Sweat created by the heat of their bodies meant they could slip and slide against each other, feeling their breasts ballooned out against each other's belly, their nipples as hard as pebbles.

Quite suddenly a new element entered the equation. Angela's fingers had lighted on the dildo. She slipped it into her hand and brought it down between Nadia's legs, pressing it into the portal of her vagina, watching as the cream plastic shell disappeared inside.

'God,' Nadia groaned. She hadn't realised it until that moment but she was missing the feeling of a hard phallus buried inside her. The vibrator was not perfect – what Nadia really wanted was a hard, hot, living cock, Hamilton's cock – but it was good enough to kick her up to another level, a higher plateau. Her sex clung to the intruder, contracting around it, and, only seconds after Angela turned it on, the vibrations reaching in to what seemed like the very centre of the sex, she came again, her body stretched taut to extract every last ounce of pleasure.

As soon as she could, as soon as the pleasure released her from its tyrannical grip, she groped between her thighs. She pushed Angela's hand away and pulled the vibrator out of her body, bringing it up to Angela's sex, the hum of its motor changing pitch as it was freed. The plastic was wet. Renewing her assault on Angela's clitoris, Nadia poked the slanting tip of the phallus into the gate of her vagina, the labia pursing around it as it sunk deep. The pitch of the humming was lowered. Nadia felt Angela's body tense, her muscles go rigid, just as hers had done, and, in seconds, she was caught in the inescapable tendrils of vibration.

'Oh God,' she gasped, the words pronounced against Nadia's sex, her breath panted out and hot. With the last of her energy she butted her tongue against Nadia's clitoris and allowed herself to be overcome in a wealth of feeling, her body convulsing, her mind blanked of everything but exquisite pleasure.

They rolled off each other and lay side by side. Slowly their heartbeats returned to normal, their breathing deepened and the sweat on their bodies dried.

Nadia was the first to speak. Getting up on one elbow she looked at the naked body of her friend and was relieved to find that she felt no regret, or shame, or anger. She felt only affection.

'I think,' she said steadily, 'the experiment was a success.'

Chapter Nine

IT HAD BEEN two weeks. He had stayed with her for four nights. She had stayed at the studio twice. They'd spent another weekend together. The rest of the time Nadia had been catching up with her sleep because sleep was difficult to come by when she was in bed with Jack Hamilton.

Her experience, the experiment with Angela, had produced no discernible effects except an over-whelming need to be fucked. That was how she thought of it. Not a need to make love but a need to be fucked. In her mind they were two different things.

Jack had obliged. Like overdosing on anything – booze, cigarettes, coffee – the most intensive period of sexual activity in her life had left her strung out, shaky and more than a little dissociated, her mind not quite able to grasp what her body was doing. But despite their over-indulgence Nadia's need had hardly slackened.

It was not all to do with Angela, of course. What had happened with Jack over the last two weeks was, she knew, just as much to blame. The depth and intensity of her sexual pleasure continued to improve and she knew it was because she was becoming emotionally, as well as physically, involved with him. That was a mistake, but he insisted as soon as his wife returned he was going to tell her he wanted a divorce. Jan Hamilton had flown from Poland to San Francisco, where she was to be photographed to promote a new range of Pandora cosmetics.

But Nadia's sexual need was primarily a physical thing. Like a toothache, it throbbed. It was so strong and robust she felt she should be able to take it out and handle it, easing the pain with her hands. Unfortunately she could do no such thing. It was buried deep inside her and could only be mitigated by a single remedy.

She parked the car and looked at the clock set in the dashboard. It was seven o'clock. She couldn't remember ever doing anything as blatant as this before but she was a different person now, different sexually, at least. The genie Hamilton had released from the bottle had grown up, become adult, established its own demands.

Getting out of the car, she was acutely aware of the silk of her dress as it rubbed against her nipples. Her imagination – the graphic images of what she was going to do – had made them hard. She wasn't wearing a bra. She wasn't wearing anything under the simple shift dress. Blatant. She had planned what she would do. The violet-coloured dress was loose. She had only to slip the shoulder straps off and it would cascade to the floor and pool at her feet. She had practised in the bedroom mirror like a child practising a curtsey for some visiting dignitary.

Her heart was pounding as she mounted the concrete steps of the mews, her bag bouncing against her hip. She rang the doorbell and unconsciously ran her tongue over her lips, making them glossy and wet. She heard footsteps on the wooden floor. Hamilton opened the door.

'Nadia,' he said with surprise, his eyes taking in every detail of her appearance. 'I thought you wanted to be alone tonight.'

'Aren't you going to ask me in?'

'Come in, of course . . .' He stepped back and she walked into the studio. 'I thought you needed to rest.'

'I changed my mind. Women's privilege.'

'Do you want a drink? That dress is wonderful. The colour's perfect with your hair.'

'Thank you, red wine would be nice.'

Nadia walked over to the easel to look at the painting. The two women in the foreground were almost complete now, one distinctly more worn-looking, a trace of world weariness in her eyes, while the other was more innocent, her face open and very much alive. It was a ravishing picture.

He got the wine from the kitchen and brought it over to her.

'Cheers,' he said, clinking his glass against the side of hers. 'So what made you change your mind?'

'It was an emergency. Needs must where the devil drives . . .' Just as she had planned she slipped the thin straps of the dress off her shoulder and it floated to the floor, the silk whispering against her body. She stepped out of the violet pool at her feet. 'I'm getting very demanding, aren't I?'

'Oh,' he said. 'I . . .' He was clearly at a loss for words.

'What's the matter, Jack? Don't tell me you're shocked?'

'No, it's just that . . . I . . . I'm all dirty. I'd like to clean up. Have a shower. Why don't I come round to your place . . .'

'Here is just fine.' He had obviously been working. His jeans and shirt were old and spattered with paint, and there was a streak of orange oil paint on his cheek. 'Well, are you going to kiss me?'

He was not usually so reluctant. All the signs were there – the way he looked at his watch, his hesitation and uneasiness. It was just that Nadia chose to ignore them.

'I'd really rather . . .'

She gagged his mouth with hers, hugging him to her, plunging her tongue between his lips, squirming her naked body against him and feeling his erection unfurl against her belly. Breaking the kiss, she dropped to her knees in front of him. She opened his flies and fished inside for his cock. It sprung free of his boxer shorts and she took it into her mouth greedily, pushing it down into her throat.

Jack took her by the shoulders and pushed her away.

'No,' he said.

'What, then?'

She ran over to the bed, threw herself down on it and opened her legs as wide as they would go. He stared at her naked body. 'You want to watch me?' she said, opening her legs and moving her hand to her sex. The heels of her shoes dug into the sheets, rucking the material around them. She had never done this for him. She let him see her finger find her clitoris, while the other hand dallied with the opening of her vagina. 'Does that excite you?'

'Yes,' he said. He was lost then. He began ripping off his clothes, his eyes riveted to Nadia's sex. 'Does it feel good?'

'It's very good.'

'You're wet. I can see it.' He knelt, naked, beside her.

She pushed first one, then two fingers into her vagina, letting him see the way her labia parted to admit them. She saw his cock pulse with excitement as the penetration made her moan.

'You like that. I can see I'm going to have to do this for you again.'

'Yes,' he replied.

She was watching his face, the look of lust she had created, a hunger as great as her own. Her body clenched with pleasure. Once she had striven and struggled to find a masturbation ritual that would bring her even a modicum of satisfaction. Now whatever she did to herself brought her to a pitch with careless ease. The instrument of her body was at last highly tuned.

Plunging her fingers in and out she strummed her clitoris with no subtlety but with considerable speed, her hand a blue of motion. She saw him glance up at her face before his eyes returned to the drama of her sex.

'Oh, oh God, what have you done to me, Jack?' she managed to say as her orgasm overtook her. She knew it would be quick. Since she had parked the car her excitement hadn't stopped building. 'Oh God.' It was the way he was looking at her that produced the final kick of pleasure. Her hands stopped moving, clutching at her sex instead as though in a desperate attempt to prevent her orgasm seeping away.

189

'Beautiful,' he said. He had forgotten the time, forgotten the other imperatives. He was engrossed in her. Without thinking he stooped and took her left ankle in his hand, easing off her shoes, kissing the top of her foot, then the slender ankle, then her calf. He kissed her thigh, up along the femur and down into the soft inner flesh. But he avoided her sex. He moved his mouth to the other leg and began a downward journey this time, kissing and nibbling and sucking every inch of her flesh. He took off her right shoe.

'Turn over,' he said as he reached her right ankle.

She rolled on to her stomach, bringing her hands up to her head, lacing her fingers together and resting her cheek against the back of them. She kept her legs wide open.

His mouth sucked on her Achilles tendon, worked up along the back of her calves and dwelt on the hollow at the back of her knee. He kissed and nibbled her thigh, tracing the crease where the top of the leg tucked into her buttock, then delved deep into the cleft of her bottom. Just as the tension of her orgasm ebbed away she was strung out again by his ministrations. His tongue explored the valley of her buttocks, but did not dip into her sex. Instead it traced along the other thigh and back down the leg to suck on the Achilles tendon of the other ankle, a journey of exploration completed, both limbs treated precisely equally.

She felt him shift on the bed, then his mouth planted itself in the small of her back, licking up along her spine. He followed the knobbly vertebrae up to her neck then worked his way out along one arm as far as the elbow, which was bent. He worked back the way he had come then over and out to the other arm. She felt his erection nudging against her shoulders. It was gorgeous. She felt her whole body coming alive.

His mouth descended to the base of her spine again, gliding over her skin with little sucking kisses. His hands caressed the two globes of her buttocks, smoothing and kneading the soft, spongy flesh as he moved to kneel between her legs.

'You're so beautiful,' he said.

'Mmm . . .'

He leant forward, lying on top of her, his cock immediately brushing against her labia. Her masturbation had made her wet but he had made her wetter, a trail of juices running on the top of her thigh.

As the crown of his cock, hot and as hard as steel, parted her labia, she felt her clitoris pulse wildly. This was what she'd come for, after all. If she were truthful with herself not an hour had gone by since she'd met Hamilton when she had not thought of him doing this to her. It was what she dreamt of and what she craved.

He held her by the hips and drove his bone-hard cock into her vagina. The feeling took her breath away, the inward plunge so long and so deep it filled her completely. He did not withdraw. He held himself there, letting her sex close around him, squeeze on him, feeling the breadth and power.

Nadia trembled. Her clitoris spasmed. The trail his mouth had left across her body was burning, as though scorched into her flesh. Every inch of it provoked her, adding to the almost unbelievable heat and passion. He was a wonderful lover. He was everything she'd ever wanted.

'Fuck me, you bastard,' she gasped, wanting

precisely that, wanting to come over his pounding cock, wanting him to take her without giving any quarter.

He pulled out. He had another surprise. Before she knew that he was doing, or could protest, his hands spread her buttocks apart. He centred his glans on the ring of her anus and, with the lubrication her own juices had provided, pushed into it. He did not penetrate far. He held himself there just long enough for her to feel an enormous jolt of sensation, then pulled out and plunged straight back into her sex, as deep as he had been before. Nadia's body spasmed in surprise. The initial shock of pain turned so quickly to pleasure, a raw, indefinable pleasure, that she cried out loud. She was melting, turning to liquid, no muscles capable of working, a delicious weakness spreading through her, speared at its centre by the hardness of his cock. As he started thrusting into her she could still feel the shadow of his erection in her rear, the nerves there tingling with an odd mixture of pain and pleasure. On the flood of these feelings her orgams washed over her, not sharp and forceful this time, but soft and mellow and incredibly deep, like a heat that penetrated through to the bone, turning her into a lake of molten lava, simmering with pleasure, seemingly without end.

'Again,' she said, once she was capable of speech.

He laughed. 'Again?'

'What have you done to me, Jack?'

She grasped his cock with the muscles of her sex and squeezed it as hard as she could. Damn Hamilton – that mantra again – damn him for reducing her to this.

Just like the last time she didn't hear the front

door open and couldn't see it from the bed. She didn't hear the footsteps across the wooden floor, though the high heels must have made quite a din. It was only when she heard the voice that she looked around in alarm.

'Well, Jack, you are being greedy.' Jan Hamilton was wearing Lycra leggings and body in a leopard skin print, her feet zipped into red patent leather ankle boots with a spiky high heel. Standing next to her was a young, petite blonde, in tight blue jeans and a dirty black T-shirt, her small breasts and large nipples clearly outlined underneath it. Jan had one arm around the blonde's shoulders. 'And I told you I was bringing you a present.'

'You're early,' Jack said with an air of resignation.

'Looks great,' the blonde giggled. 'I love it.' She peeled off the T-shirt, kicked off her scuffed, black leather high heels and began unzipping her jeans. Her eyes were roaming Nadia's body.

Nadia struggled to roll out from under Jack. Before she could stop her the blonde had sat on the edge of the bed and cupped Nadia's left breast in her hand. Nadia slapped it away instantly, the heat of her breast turned suddenly to ice.

'That's not very friendly,' the blonde said in a voice with a Cockney accent. She moved her hand to Jack's erection. He did not react. The blonde crawled forward. 'Lovely big cock, just like you said,' she told Jan before sucking it into her mouth.

Despite herself Nadia felt a pulse of desire. She scrambled to her feet.

'Don't go, honey,' Jan said, catching her arm. 'If I'd known you were going to be here I wouldn't have brought Eve. But there's plenty to go round. You know Jack.'

Nadia knew Jack. She shook Jan's arm off, picked up her dress and pulled it over her head. She collected her shoes and bag, and marched to the front door, slamming it closed after her. She didn't put her shoes on until she was standing beside her car.

The anger was transitory. As she got behind the wheel she felt remarkably calm. There was no decision to make, no agonising over what she should do, what would be right or wrong. Jack had made that decision for her.

The Guildhall sparkled like the inside of a jewel. Silver candlesticks stood on every table, the polished Georgian silver catching the light from the crystal chandeliers. The dresses of most of the women, too, and their diamonds, glittered and twinkled in contrast to the plain black and white of the men's formal suits.

After the long, indigestible and – by virtue of the fact that the kitchens were so far from the long lines of tables – partially cold meal, the speeches too appeared interminable. Nadia had looked at her watch several times and on each occasion it gave her the sad news that the event was nowhere near its completion. James Hill, on the other hand, who had insisted on her coming to the banquet, appeared content to listen to the pontifications from the top table, though he had sequestered his own bottle of Remy Martin to refill his frequently empty glass.

Eventually it was over. The last speaker sat down to a chorus of polite applause, frock-coated waiters served the last of the coffee and people began drifting away, a fleet of chauffeur-driven cars lining the street outside.

194

When he got to his feet James Hill discovered he was a little the worse for wear and headed off to the toilet, leaving Nadia in the anteroom outside the dining room.

'Hello.' He had come up behind her without her being aware of it. She spun round to face Andrew Anderson.

'Andrew.' She was surprised. She hadn't seen him in the dining room. 'I didn't know you were here.'

'That's a beautiful dress.' It was. The strapless boned bodice in a crimson satin clung to Nadia's bosom. It was shaped into her waist and finished in a little peplum on her hips, under which the ankle-length skirt stretched tightly over the rich curves of her buttocks and thighs.

'Thank you,' she said, not quite sure how Andrew was going to react. She had aborted the trip to Rome with the flimsiest of excuses and since then had not returned any of his calls. He had very quickly got the message that he was surplus to requirements.

'And you look stunning, Nadia,' he said earnestly. 'I mean it.'

'That's very nice of you.'

There was a silence, neither quite sure what they wanted to say next.

'I . . .'

'It was . . .' They both spoke at once.

'Go ahead,' he said.

'I was going to call you,' she said weakly. 'I didn't behave very well, did I?'

'No,' he said, smiling, 'but it doesn't matter. It's just nice to see you again. You're here with James, aren't you?'

'Yes.' She suddenly wondered if this whole thing

had been engineered, if Anderson had persuaded Hill to bring her. 'But he's suffering from an overdose of Remy Martin.'

'Can I take you home then?'

It had been four weeks since she had seen Anderson. Her experience with Hamilton had wiped the memory of him away. She remembered telling Angela that, if she had not met Jack, she would have felt differently about Andrew. She wondered if that was true.

'That would be very nice,' she said and discovered she meant it.

They found James Hill, who was delighted the Hill Brothers' Jaguar was not going to have to take a detour to Islington. He appeared totally uninterested as to why Nadia should want to go off with Anderson and accepted his explanation that her house was on his way home, though if he had cared to think about it, it was not.

'Would you do me a favour?' Nadia said as they settled into the back of a chauffeur-driven Rolls Royce.

'Of course.'

'Would you take me for a drink first? I don't feel like going home yet.'

'It's gone midnight. Most bars are closed. What about my place?'

'Fine. If you don't mind.'

'It's not far.'

Anderson had the penthouse flat in a mansion block just off Cadogan Square. It was vast, with tall ceilings and large, imposing rooms, all decorated with meticulous attention to detail. The furniture was an eclectic mixture of antique and modern, and the paintings that littered the walls were equally varied, from Russian icons and Victorian landscapes to abstracts by Hartung and Rothko. The living room, which had a spectacular view of London, was lined with oak shelves crammed with books. In the kitchen, fitted by Gaggenau in black and stainless steel, Anderson put on the coffee and poured Nadia an Armagnac.

'Can I ask you why you didn't return my calls?' he asked tentatively.

'I was taking the coward's way out. I'm sorry. It was rude.'

'It's all right. It was my fault.' He was looking at the stream of liquid filtering into the coffee jug.

'How was it your fault?'

'I know my limitations.'

'Limitations? What limitations?'

'Sexual limitations.'

'Is that what you think? Do you think the reason I didn't call you was because of what happened in bed?'

'You know it is.'

'Andrew. Please. I enjoyed our sex.' It was true but not the whole truth.

'Really?'

The coffee machine finished. Anderson took the pot and two cups and saucers and put them on a tray together with the bottle of Armagnac, then led her through into the living room. They sat side by side on a large, comfortable sofa.

'The reason I didn't call was that I got involved with someone else.' She decided she should tell him the truth. 'I told you I'd had an affair?'

'Yes.'

'Well, it broke out again.'

'The same man?'

'Yes, and I made the same mistake. It was a disaster.'

'I wish you'd called me.'

'I just thought it was a bit much . . .'

'I'd have understood. I do understand.'

In the short time they had been together Nadia's feelings for Anderson had rekindled. There was a certain lack of masculinity about him that was positively refreshing after Hamilton. On impulse she leant forward and kissed him on the cheek. Before she could pull away again he caught her face in his hand and kissed her on the mouth. His tongue darted hesitantly between her' lips and before she knew what she was doing she found herself sucking it in hungrily.

Pulling herself up, Nadia got to her feet. She walked over and examined a Paul Nash landscape that hung on the opposite wall, wanting to give herself time to sort out her feelings. She felt Anderson's eyes watching her but he said nothing.

She tried to analyse what she felt about Andrew. Of course she had been tempted to call him soon after the debacle with Hamilton, to let his company and his wealth distract her, to allow good food, fine wines and visits to the opera and theatre wash away her sense of disappointment. But the reason she had hesitated was not only because she had thought he might take a jaundiced view of her sudden change of heart. It was something more fundamental. What he had said in the kitchen was true. Their sexual encounter had been limited.

Perhaps before she had met Hamilton she would not have minded – it was possible she would not even have noticed. But there was no turning back the clock. Hamilton had charged her sexuality and she had no intention of returning to the good old, bad days. Sex, for her, had become like an unexplored desert island. She had already started to chart its territory, map out its hills and climb some of its mountains. She had no intention of going back to the beach, getting on the boat and rowing away.

If she was going to have a relationship with Anderson then the "limitations" as he had called them had to be dealt with. She turned and walked back to the sofa, sitting down next to him and taking a sip of her Vieux Armagnac.

'A lot has happened to me recently, Andrew,' she said. She crossed her legs, making the satin rustle. She saw him looking at her black suede high heels. The strap over the arch of her foot was decorated with diamanté. 'I've realised that for a lot of my life I have accepted compromises in my relationships. I've been prepared to settle for things I should not have done. Can you understand that?'

'I think so.'

'Well, I've decided I need to change that. I'm not going to compromise any more.'

'I understand that.'

'What you said in the kitchen . . . about sex, I mean. Do you want the truth?'

He looked a little frightened but he nodded.

'I had the feeling you were holding back. If we're going to have any sort of relationship you have to be honest with me about what you want.'

'You might not care for it.'

'That's true, but then at least we'd know, and we wouldn't be fumbling about in the dark pretending.' It was odd, she thought, how her new sexuality seemed to have made her assertive, too. It was a trait she'd admired in Angela but been unable to exercise herself – until now. 'Do you agree?'

He didn't reply. There was a long silence as he stared down into his lap.

'Perhaps this is a mistake,' Nadia said finally.

'No. No, you are absolutely right. I know you are. What is the point in fudging around things?' He looked up and into her eyes and she could see him taking a deep breath. 'There *are* certain things I like, I need, in bed, things I find difficult to ask for.'

'I'm very open-minded, Andrew.' She wondered if that was true.

'Are you?' An expression of anguish was etched on his face. He searched her eyes as if looking for some clue as to how she might react.

'Tell me what you want.'

'I've always had this problem, Nadia. I've had to live with it.'

'You were married . . .'

'Oh, my wife made it quite clear she wasn't going to help, and she didn't know the half of it.' Anderson sat up, took a sip of coffee and looked at her intensely. The expression in his eyes had changed. Nadia could see he had made a decision. 'You really want this, don't you?'

'I told you, Andrew, there is no point in a compromise.'

'It has to be now. I couldn't spend two or three days thinking about it, worrying about it.'

When Nadia had asked him to take her for a drink she hadn't had the slightest intention of going to bed with him. But then she hadn't had the slightest intention of having this conversation either.

'I can understand that,' she said. 'I'm not going anywhere.'

'You'll have to give me twenty minutes.'

'What do you mean?'

'If you want to know about me, Nadia, it's better I show you.'

'All right,' she said, trying to sound positive.

'Twenty minutes.'

He got to his feet and strode out of the room without looking back, afraid the slightest hesitation might change his mind.

Nadia finished her Armagnac, poured another coffee and wandered around the room. Glancing at the small brass carriage clock on one of the book shelves, she saw it was eleven-ten. She listened intently for any clue to what was going on but could hear nothing.

The trouble was, of course, she hadn't expected this reaction. She had expected him to respond either by telling her that he realised there was a problem and that there was nothing he could do about it, or by saying that they would work on it together to make it right. But clearly, she thought, as she roamed the room looking at the paintings, fingering the objects d'art, without seeing or feeling either, Anderson had some sort of perverse fetish. He wanted to be whipped or tied to the bed. Nadia hardly knew what to expect.

The twenty minutes passed slowly. At eleven-thirty Nadia drank the last of the coffee, then ventured down the hall. He hadn't told her where the bedroom was and all the doors in the long corridor were closed. She tried the first one to the left and discovered an elaborate bathroom. The next door down on the right was a small guest room decorated in a flowery wallpaper.

There were two doors at the far end of the hall. She tried the first, which opened on to a large bedroom. The decor was a symphony of blues: heavy drapes over the big windows, the bed stripped back to a pale blue undersheet, and the light from the dark blue shades of the bedside lamps dimmed to a pleasant glow.

But Nadia thought she must be in the wrong room. Sitting on the edge of the bed in a long-sleeved, polo-necked cream silk cocktail dress was a pretty, fair-haired woman. Her legs were sheathed in tan-coloured nylon and she was wearing cream suede shoes with an ankle strap. She had three rings on her left hand and a gold bracelet sparking with diamonds on her right wrist. Her make-up was heavy, a thick pancake, with eyelashes that were clearly artificial, dark eye shadow and very red lipstick. Her hair was permed in an old-fashioned style, curls framing her face right down to her shoulders.

It took Nadia minutes before the penny dropped. Suddenly she realised the hair was a wig and the "woman" was Andrew Anderson.

'My God,' she said under her breath.

'I'm not homosexual,' he said firmly.

Nadia wasn't at all sure what her reaction was. Her initial surprise became horror, then turned to fascination. She studied Andrew's face, trying to see his masculinity behind the mask of what was a totally feminine appearance. He made a very convincing woman, his small-featured face and slight body fitting the role perfectly. His legs were slender and shapely and his ankles and feet dainty in the high heels.

'You're beautiful,' Nadia said, meaning it.

'Thank you.' She had obviously said the right thing. The remark gave him confidence. 'Are you shocked?'

'Of course,' she said. She was remembering how he had handled her clothes so carefully. Had he been imagining how they would feel on him?

'I've never let anyone see me like this,' he said.

Nadia sat on the bed beside him. 'What do you want me to do?' she said. She put her hand on his knee, rubbing her fingers against the silk and the nylon. She'd thought it odd that he had such hairless legs; now she wondered if he shaved them.

'I'm not homosexual,' he repeated. 'I only want to have sex with a woman.'

'Dressed like this.'

'Yes. I just love the feel, the softness. I always have. My wife caught me one day putting on some tights. That was the end. She'd never have sex with me again.'

Well, Nadia thought, she had asked for it. She'd asked him to tell her the truth and now she had the truth in spades. He'd exposed himself to her completely, holding nothing back. Now she had to make a choice. She could get up and walk out. She could say, politely, thank you but no thank you and walk away. Or she could stay. Whatever she did she knew she must be careful. Andrew's secrets were laid open and he was as vulnerable, emotionally, as he would ever be.

'You'll have to help me, Andrew,' she said finally. 'I've never . . .'

He put his arm around her. Experimentally he kissed her on the mouth, very lightly, without using his tongue. The silk of his dress rustled against the satin of her own. She felt his obviously padded bosom crushing her breast on her left side. Putting her hand around his neck under the wig she pulled his lips on to hers more fiercely, putting her tongue

203

into his mouth.

'What do I call you?' she said. It appeared she had decided to go through with it.

'Andrea.'

Nadia got to her feet, the range of emotions she felt still not focused on any one. She felt sympathy and compasion, a strong streak of absurdity and more than a little excitement. She felt no disgust.

'Are you going to take your dress off, Andrea?' Nadia reached behind her back and undid the long zip of her dress.

'Yes,' he said, his eyes looking at her with a mixture of gratitude and apprehension. He got up and stripped the dress off, draping it, as carefully as he had once dealt with Nadia's clothes, over a small button-backed armchair. He was wearing a tight, white all-in-one corset with satin shoulder straps and a diamond-shaped satin panel over his navel. Suspenders from the base of the corset held up tan stockings, pulling the tops into chevrons on his thighs. The bra of the corset contained two flesh-coloured flexible plastic bags which looked to be filled with some sort of liquid. A small pair of white French knickers covered his crotch but Nadia could see his erection outlined underneath them.

'Pretty,' she said. She felt a strong pulse of desire as she looked at the bulge in the knickers.

'Thank you.'

'You want to do it like this?' she asked.

'It's ridiculous, isn't it?' The shame-faced expression she had seen on their first night together returned.

'No,' she said forcibly. She stood in front of him. 'I want you. I want you to fuck me. Let's not think about anything else.' It was true. The shock and surprise of all this had apparently not affected her basic instincts. She kicked off her shoes and pulled her dress from her shoulders, stepping out of it. She draped it over the chair Andrew had used for his dress. Brusquely she unclipped her bra, stripped her tights down to her knees then sat on the bed to roll them off her legs completely. She wore no panties.

'I haven't worn stockings for ages,' she said.

'I love them. They feel so sexy,' he said in an uncharacteristically light voice.

'Do you shave your legs?'

'Only a bit. I've never had much hair.'

'I always have to shave mine.'

'You don't have to shave your face,' he replied with what sounded a little like envy.

'Are you going to lie back now, Andrea? Let me get at you.'

'Yes,' he said breathily.

'Come on then. Come on, Andrea.'

She could see the name gave him a frisson of excitement. He squirmed back into the centre of the bed. Nadia ran her hand up his leg to the French knickers. The sac of his balls was confined tightly under their gusset. She ran her hand over it and he moaned.

'Shall I take your panties off, Andrea?'

'Please . . .'

She pulled the waistband over the corset as he raised his hips, and skimmed the knickers down his legs. They caught on the ankle strap of his shoes but she disentangled them carefully then threw them aside. His erection had embedded itself under the front of the corset and she had to pull it out. Unsurprisingly it was harder and bigger than it had been before.

'Oh, darling . . .' he moaned at her touch.

'You have to fuck me hard, Andrea,' she said, meaning it.

'I will.'

Nadia knew she was already moist. There was undoubtedly something erotic about this bizarre situation. She gave up trying to work out how it could be sexually exciting for a man to want to have sex with a woman, dressed in woman's clothes, but exciting it clearly was. Anderson's cock was throbbing visibly.

She swung her thigh over Anderson's hip. Her breasts quivered. She settled the tip of his glans between her labia and felt her own wetness leaking from her body. She looked down at Anderson, for all intents and purposes a woman, a woman with a cock but a woman nonetheless.

Was that it? Nadia thought. Was that why she was not revolted or turned off by all this, because she had learned to express desire for a woman without fear? She felt her sex throb as she remembered the almost impossible softness of Angela's body against her own.

She realised she couldn't see Andrew Anderson any more, could not make the intellectual leap of looking through the woman she saw in front of her eyes to the man who had sat with her thirty minutes before. There was no need. She was quite content with the woman. She leant forward and traced the contours of a woman's face with her finger. She ran the tip of one finger over a woman's lips.

'Lovely,' she said.

The word made Anderson's cock pulse.

A woman with a cock. She allowed her body to drop, falling on to the hard shaft. Anderson moved his hands to his sides, smoothing them against the corset.

'Hard,' she said. Pressing herself down on him she was completely confused now. Was the swelling, increasing urgent desire she was feeling for a man or for a woman? Did it really matter? It was the same thing, the same result, her body already seized by the rhythms of orgasm. Wasn't that what Angela had said – it was all the same thing?

He began pumping into her, bucking his hips, forcing his cock up into her, moving his hands on to her thighs to hold her down on him, grinding his pubic bone against her clitoris. His cock was like a rod of steel.

'Yes . . . yes . . .' she cried.

His body strained against the tight corset, the suspenders pulling at the stockings as he squirmed deeper.

It was a contradiction, a contradiction of opposites. Andrew's hardness at the centre of her sex, and his femininity surrounding it, the one caused by the other. Giving up any attempt to sort them out, Nadia simply surrendered to her feelings, getting her excitement from the woman who lay underneath her *and* from the man who pumped away inside her. She felt her sex spasming, contracting around the shaft of the flesh that invaded it and sending a wave of sensation up through her body, enveloping her like a rising tide, forcing her eyes to roll back, blacking out the vision of a woman and making her concentrate on the essence of a man. As she wriggled and writhed to the dictates of her orgasm Andrew pounded on, faster and harder, sensing her pleasure, feeling the top of her sex melting because of it, opening for him, giving him space to shoot his seed. The walls of her vagina were as silky and smooth as the clothes he loved to wear.

He stopped, held her thighs tightly with fingers of steel and came, his body trembling, the female clothing clinging and coaxing his flesh, the sound of his name (his real name, what he wanted to be) on her lips.

'Andrea,' Nadia cried as she felt him climax inside her.

'It's quite common, apparently. I read up about it.'

'Really? I thought it was just gays.'

'They're not gay at all. They want to have completely normal heterosexual relationships.'

'Wearing women's clothes?'

'Exactly.'

'Weird. I think I can understand a man wanting to be a woman, wanting to have his dick cut off and all that. But logically, in the end, he'd be having sex with a man.'

'That's transsexualism,' Nadia said. 'Transvestites are different. They just like the touch and feel of women's clothes. That's their turn-on.'

'And you used to say I was the one who always got the weirdos,' Angela said. It was true. For once it was Nadia with a long story of a sexual adventure, spiced with sexual foibles.

'B H I would have run a mile.'

'B H?'

'Before Hamilton . . .'

'But you didn't.'

'I told you. It was quite sexy in a peculiar sort of way; I suppose mostly because he was so turned on.'

'But it wasn't like having sex with Hamilton?'

'Nothing's like that, Angela.'

'You lucky bitch. He's just my type, too. Why didn't I go to that bloody exhibition? Anyway, what are you going to do?'

'About Anderson?'

'Of course about Anderson.'

They were sitting out in Nadia's patio garden. It was Sunday evening and, according to the weather forecast, had been the hottest day in London since records began. The television news had shown pictures of thousands of people lying head to toe in Hyde Park, girls diving topless into the Serpentine and eggs being fried on the pavements in Oxford Street. Even now, with the sun low in the sky, heat radiated from the stone flags of the patio and the walls of the house and it was impossible to get cool.

Nadia got up and refilled their glasses. They were drinking from a carafe of white wine and lemon juice Nadia had mixed and left to marinade in the fridge overnight.

'You know what I'm going to do.'

'How extensive is his wardrobe? Perhaps he's got some nice dresses you could borrow.'

'It's not funny. I just couldn't face it.'

'You said it was exciting.'

'I said it was peculiar. It was the sort of excitement you get when you've stolen a sweet from a sweet shop. It tastes better because it's stolen, but you know it's wrong. I feel sorry for him but that's not the basis for a relationship.'

'He's very rich, Nadia.'

'What difference does that make?'

Angela was laughing. 'You could go on a shopping spree together. Get him to take you to Fifth Avenue, or the Via Condotti.'

'Be serious.'

'Have you told him?'

'I told him on Friday. He was expecting it. To tell you the truth I wish I could have been more understanding. I like him.'

'And Hamilton? What are you going to do about Hamilton?'

The answer was not as simple as it would have been had Angela asked the question immediately after Nadia's last visit to his studio. Then she would have said that she had no intention of ever seeing him again. But since her night with Andrew/Andrea she had been thinking a lot about Hamilton.

Previously, she had assumed that in order to have a sexually meaningful relationship with a man she also had to have an emotional commitment to him. Since the emotional commitment had never materialised – except in the case of her married man, when she had fought tooth and nail not to become involved with him – she had drawn the conclusion that this was the base cause for her sexual inadequacies. She had reasoned from this that unless there was a chance of an emotional commitment developing in a relationship there would be no chance of sexual fulfilment. Having sex with a man who meant nothing to her would therefore be fruitless. Casual sex, for her, unlike Angela, had always been ruled out.

The force of Hamilton's personality, or the sheer physical attraction she had felt for him, or both, had broken the mould. But she had assumed that because they had great sex, they also had to have an emotional commitment. She had kidded herself that she was falling in love with Hamilton, but the fact was that all she actually felt for him was unmitigated lust. She was immensely relieved to find she was not in love with him.

If she were honest with herself, what she had felt when Jan Hamilton had arrived at the studio with the blonde had been, quite simply, nothing. But she had reacted as if she had been rejected. She'd acted as though she were jealous. Hamilton, of course, had compounded this travesty by pretending he wanted to leave his wife. Even if he had been genuine in that desire, Nadia should have realised that he would find it impossible to give up the sort of sexual menu his wife was offering him.

What her experience with Tony and the bizarre experience with Andrew had taught her – to say nothing of what had happened with Angela – was that there was no connection between sex and emotion. She had been able to indulge Andrew's outré tastes and enjoy herself and yet feel no emotional ties. Conversely the opposite would not have been true. If she had cared for Andrew, if she had fallen in love with him, her ability to cope with his revelations would have been severely limited. It was not caring that had freed her.

So it was with Hamilton. In the beginning, in the gallery where she had propositioned him so brazenly, she didn't know him or care about him. It hadn't spoiled her enjoyment; in fact, she realised, by the same token it had enabled her to be totally uninhibited.

The truth was that, as much as she had tried subsequently to persuade herself that she cared for Hamilton, based on a perverse misunderstanding of her own psychology, she could never do so. She had run away from him because she feared a repeat of what had happened with her other married man. But she knew now she would never become involved with Hamilton in that way. There was therefore, she had concluded with a certain amount of glee, nothing to stop her using Hamilton for her own purposes, using being the operative word.

'I wanted to talk to you about that,' Nadia said in answer to Angela's question. 'There was something I had in mind.'

'Tell me more.'

'Let's eat, I'm starving,' Nadia said. She had two large cold lobsters in the fridge and had prepared a salad of lettuce, mache and rocket.

'Me too,' Angela agreed.

They walked into the house together.

Nadia's feelings for her friend, she was glad to say, had not been changed by their intimacy. Both had enjoyed the experience. For Nadia it had played an important part in sorting out her sexuality. It had even occurred to her that the fear she had hidden for so long over what had happened with Barbara was partly responsible for her sexual hiatus. Whether that was true or not, she had confronted her fear and used Angela as a way of sorting herself out. How big a part women would play in her future sexuality she had no idea. At least she had no idea in the long term. In the short term she knew more or less precisely.

Angela sat at the table as Nadia laid out the food. She opened a bottle of Chablis and poured it into the glass she had set on the table.

'So,' Angela said. 'Are you going to tell me what you've got in mind?'

The front doorbell rang at exactly the prescribed hour. It was getting dark, the summer evening beginning to pull in. Nadia had watched Jack Hamilton get out of a taxi from her bedroom window. She still felt the same pulse of excitement she had always felt every time she had seen him. But this was different. This was on her terms.

He'd sounded puzzled on the phone. He tried to apologise and invent some explanation for what had happened and was obviously nonplussed when Nadia appeared totally uninterested. She'd asked him if he wanted to come round to her house that night. He'd said he did. He'd said he couldn't think of anything he'd rather do.

Nadia walked downstairs slowly. She was wearing a black lace teddy cut so high on the hips it revealed most of the crease of her pelvis. It also gave tantalising glimpses of her breasts under its lacy cups. Her nipples were so hard they felt like round glass beads.

'Come in,' she said, opening the front door.

Hamilton walked inside, not smiling, his eyes riveted to her body. He was wearing a pair of beige cotton slacks, and a white shirt. The front of his black hair fell on to his forehead and he flicked it back with a characteristic gesture. 'You look wonderful,' he said.

'Thank you, I thought you'd appreciate it.'

'Look, I know I owe you an explanation . . .'

'Jack, you owe me nothing.'

'It's just . . .'

'Sh . . .' She put her finger to his lips. They felt hot. She ran her finger across his mouth then pushed it between his lips. 'Aren't you going to kiss me?'

He wrapped his arms around her, his hands caressing the silky nylon of the teddy as his mouth closed over hers. He kissed her hard, hugging her to his strong body, his cock immediately unfurling against her belly.

Nadia felt her body throb. She pushed her mons

against his erection, letting a wave of sexual energy wash over her.

'Come with me,' she said, finally breaking away. 'I've got a present for you.'

She took his hand and led him upstairs, making him follow her so his eyes could feast on her long legs and her buttocks, neatly bisected by the black material. Her excitement was compounded by the fact that she was in control, that this was her scenario they were playing out.

Outside the bedroom door, which was firmly closed, she turned around, resting her back against it.

'What is it?' he said.

'I told you, I've got a present for you.'

'A present from you is the last thing I expected, Nadia.'

'I owe you a lot, Jack. More than you will ever know.' She meant it because it was the truth. She reached out her hand and touched the bulge in his flies but when he tried to kiss her again she twisted away. 'Open the door,' she said.

He turned the handle of the door and went in. The curtains were drawn and the bedside lamp, draped with a red scarf, cast a dim but rosy glow. There was enough light to see Angela clearly. She was lying on the bed naked apart from a pair of tiny black silk panties that barely covered her thick growth of red pubic hair. She was holding the cream plastic vibrator to her lips, licking it like an ice cream cone.

'I almost started without you,' she said.

WARNING: These books are *X Rated* . . .

PRIVATE ACT
Zara Devereux

'She was completely powerless under Gerard's domination, with no responsibility, no say in what was done to her. He tied her wrists together with a scarf and secured them to the legs of the stool, then set about tethering her ankles . . .'

Kasia Lyndon is a good-looking but struggling young actress who is thrilled to get her first break at the Craven Playhouse, a privately owned theatre company in a country manor house.

But this is no ordinary theatre, and she must live her role both on and off stage – even when it demands that she submits herself to her sadistic leading man and his mistress. Kasia, however, soon discovers that this domination has unleashed feelings in her that she never dreamt she had.

THE DOMINATRIX
Emma Allan

> '*Karen looked in the mirror again. She hardly recognised herself. The tight basque, the stockings and the high-heeled shoes had transformed her body. Her breasts looked yielding and impossibly creamy in contrast to the shiny red satin. She looked like an expensive whore . . .*'

Karen Masters has never been very interested in sex. But when she sees a video of her friend Barbara engaging in some very *outré* sex games with her husband Dan, she begins to realise what she has been missing.

Beautiful redhead Pamela Stern is a dominatrix and more than willing to show Karen exactly what this means. As she wields the whip Karen's sexuality comes alive, and when she discovers that one of Pamela's clients is her own boss Malcolm Travers, she agrees to become his personal dominatrix. Now Karen can fully explore the limits of her own desires, at least until Malcolm's wife finds out . . .

HOUSE OF DECADENCE
Lucia Cubelli

*'Why do you keep tormenting me?' she moaned,
as his hand left her breasts and crept down
between her spread thighs.*

*'Because I love watching you struggle as you
learn each lesson,' explained Fabrizio. 'I want to
teach you everything there is to know about sex. I
promised you that your life would change if you
came here, and I always keep my promises.'*

At 23, Megan Stewart feels there should be more
to life than working in a public library so she
answers an advert for a post in a country house –
and discovers what she has been missing.

Handsome Fabrizio Balocchi is far from his
Tuscan home and feeling bored. But he instinctively knows that Megan will be a natural player
in his games of domination and, step by step, he
leads her into a darker world, a world where
pleasure is mixed with pain. Now Megan must
decide how far she is willing to go in order to
stay in Fabrizio's house of decadence . . .

Other X-rated fiction, available by mail: